"Lately, I feel like someone is watching me."

"Did this start before you found the note?" Dex asked Katrina.

"Yes. I thought it was all in my head. But now I'm not so sure."

Giving Katrina a false sense of security would not be a smart move. But having her afraid of her own shadow was not the way to go either. "I wouldn't read too much into it." Dex warned, "But keep your eyes open, and don't let your guard down."

Katrina smiled. "I'll try not to."

Dex noticed a ringlet of hair had fallen across Katrina's brow. Without giving it a thought, he touched her soft skin, feeling a jolt in return. Did she feel it too as he tucked the errant strand behind her ear?

She blushed. "Thanks for noticing."

"My pleasure." He grinned. Their eyes locked for a long moment of connection before Dex did the only sensible thing he could. He walked away while he was still able to...

CAPTURED ON KAUAI

R. BARRI FLOWERS

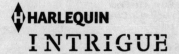

HARLEQUIN

INTRIGUE

In memory of my beloved mother, Marjah Aljean, a lifelong
fan of Harlequin romances, who provided me the tools needed
to find success in both my professional and personal lives. To
Loraine, the one and only love of my life, whose support has
been steadfast through the many years together. And to the
loyal fans of my romance, mystery, suspense and thriller fiction
published over the years. Lastly, a nod goes out to my super
editors, Allison Lyons and Denise Zaza, for the opportunity to
become a valued part of the Harlequin Intrigue family.

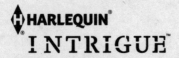

Recycling programs
for this product may
not exist in your area.

ISBN-13: 978-1-335-58220-1

Captured on Kauai

Copyright © 2022 by R. Barri Flowers

For questions and comments about the quality of this book,
please contact us at CustomerService@Harlequin.com.

Harlequin Enterprises ULC
22 Adelaide St. West, 41st Floor
Toronto, Ontario M5H 4E3, Canada
www.Harlequin.com

Printed in U.S.A.

R. Barri Flowers is an award-winning author of crime, thriller, mystery and romance fiction featuring three-dimensional protagonists, riveting plots, unexpected twists and turns, and heart-pounding climaxes. With an expertise in true crime, serial killers and characterizing dangerous offenders, he is perfectly suited for the Harlequin Intrigue line. Chemistry and conflict between the hero and heroine, attention to detail and incorporating the very latest advances in criminal investigations are the cornerstones of his romantic suspense fiction. Discover more on popular social networks and Wikipedia.

Books by R. Barri Flowers

Harlequin Intrigue

Hawaii CI

The Big Island Killer
Captured on Kauai

Chasing the Violet Killer

Visit the Author Profile page at Harlequin.com.

CAST OF CHARACTERS

Dex Adair—The DEA special agent goes undercover at the Maoli Lodge on Kauai along with his narcotics-detector golden retriever, Barnabas, to investigate the death of a fellow agent and a possible illicit drug-trafficking operation. He hadn't intended to fall for the lodge proprietor and want to protect her from a stalker.

Katrina Sizemore—A widow and owner of the Maoli Lodge, she begins receiving notes that suggest the death of her late husband, Joseph, was not an accident, and she turns to her new pianist, Dex, for help. Can they learn to trust each other and open their hearts with deadly traffickers in their midst?

Roxanne Yamamoto—The DEA agent died in a mysterious car accident while undercover. Can she still help in the investigation and expose her killer even from the grave?

Alyson Tennison—As the assistant manager at the lodge, is she the steady hand Katrina needs in running the resort effectively, or is she hiding something?

Clayton Pietz—The Kauai PD vice section detective heads investigations into illegal drug trafficking on the Hawaiian island. Can he break up the drug operation before another person dies?

Lynda Krause—A DEA agent who is driven to help nail Roxanne's killer and go after the deadly traffickers of illegal drugs.

Prologue

Her cover had been blown. DEA Agent Roxanne Yamamoto tensed behind the wheel of her Toyota Tacoma as she drove down Kaumualii Highway in the dark of night. Was she being followed? Or was it just her overactive imagination after having to flee for her life? She had a story to tell, one that Roxanne's colleagues in the United States Drug Enforcement Administration would definitely want to hear. As an intelligence research specialist, her job was to identify and analyze the manufacturing, distribution and trafficking of narcotics, wherever it was happening, and start the process of dismantling the criminal networks. While working undercover in her latest assignment, it had taken her to the Hawaiian island of Kauai. Its moniker, the "Garden Isle," was apropos, with awesome tropical rainforests and a lush landscape comprising much of the island. If only she were afforded the time to take it all in, instead of being on assignment, trying to put the brakes on one branch of a Western United States drug-trafficking network that marred paradise with its ugliness, turning people into addicts and criminals. Maybe someday.

Roxanne's thoughts turned back to the unsettling moment at hand. She was able to get enough incriminating information to lead to a full-scale investigation and some arrests. Turned out that the leads they followed proved productive in targeting the operation and some of its operatives. If she survived this, it would no doubt be a feather in her cap and lead to bigger and better assignments. Maybe she would take some time off and work on her love life, which was sorely lacking at the moment, having broken up with her cheating boyfriend six months ago. Or maybe she was better off without all the drama relationships seemed to bring like a daytime soap opera.

Again, she looked up at the rearview mirror to see if anyone was on her tail. No one. Or was this meant to somehow give her a false sense of security now that she had seemingly managed to get away while still in one piece? She reached into the pocket of her flare jeans for her cell phone, needing to let other members of the Drug Task Force assigned to the case know she was in trouble. It wasn't there. Damn. In her haste to get away, she must have left the phone at the cottage she was renting when escaping from her pursuers through the back door. Also left behind was her laptop containing crucial information and incriminating evidence in the investigation.

Only then did Roxanne spot the bright car lights from behind. Someone was following her. And gain-ing ground. She couldn't make out the driver. Panicked, she increased her own speed, noting that there was virtually no traffic at this time of night to slow her down. She reached down to her waist holster and felt the cold steel of her Glock 17 duty pistol. This gave her some comfort, knowing if push came to shove she might need to use it in self-defense against the enemy.

After she had managed to put some distance between her and the other vehicle, Roxanne's sense of comfort faded quickly, as the other car rapidly caught up to her. Again, she picked up her speed, hoping to escape to safety. When the pursuer inexplicably slowed down, for a brief moment she wondered if the chase had been entirely in her head. Only upon realizing she was going way too fast to maneuver the car safely, did Roxanne press down on the brakes. Instead of the car decreasing speed, it was just the opposite. She slammed her foot on the brakes again and realized that they weren't working. Had they been tampered with?

I have to get through this, she thought with determination. But before she could attempt to find some way to bring the car to a stop and continue to live her life and build upon her career, Roxanne lost control of the vehicle, crashing into a utility pole with blunt force. There was nothing after that.

Chapter One

DEA special agent Dex Adair prepared to enter the warehouse in Downtown Los Angeles. He and the team of other agents and members of the Los Angeles County Sheriff's Narcotic Bureau, armed with Glocks, Rock River Arms LAR-15 semiautomatic carbines and Remington 870 12-gauge shotguns, stormed the building. They were in search of illegal marijuana, following a months-long investigation of a crime syndicate that had trafficked drugs in California, Nevada and Hawaii. It was a reflection of the flourishing black market in existence for drugs, despite the legality of recreational marijuana in some states and elsewhere.

Dex expected resistance, knowing those operating the lucrative illicit business were unlikely to give up and spend years, if not decades, in prison without a major fight. *Bring it on*, he thought, no stranger to danger and facing perilous predicaments in life. Having grown up in the sometimes mean streets of the Motor City, otherwise known as Detroit, day-to-day survival was anything but a given to young African American males. But survive he did, motivated to do so in picking up his bachelor's and master's degrees in criminal justice from Michigan State University, before building a successful career in law enforcement within the United States Department of Justice. At thirty-three and six feet three inches of solid muscle, he was more than capable of holding his own when duty called. So was his trusty companion, Barnabas, a narcotic detection service dog. The male golden retriever, part of a K-9 unit, was reliable in sniffing out illicit drugs. He didn't take kindly to being attacked and could defend himself, and then some, including coming to the rescue of his fellow law enforcement officers. Still, Dex kept the canine safely outside for the time being as the agents and detectives fanned out, catching the suspects off guard and ill prepared to take on the massive presence and firepower they encountered. When it was over, there were casualties on the side of the bad guys, while the good guys emerged virtually unscathed.

Once arrests were made and the building secured, Dex stepped out and returned with Barnabas. He unleashed the canine in the spacious warehouse and allowed him to do his thing. It paid off big-time. "We've got something," Dex called out excitedly to the team as his hard, coal-gray eyes focused on the pallets attracting the attention of Barnabas.

"Don't keep us in suspense, Adair," Agent Lynda Krause snapped with anticipation. The long-legged, green-eyed forty-year-old had a short, platinum layered bob and an attitude befitting her seventeen years with the DEA. "What do we get for our trouble?"

Dex grinned and scratched his forehead, if only to keep her waiting a little longer, before donning vinyl disposable gloves. He grabbed a crowbar left behind by the perps and ripped open a pallet, causing his eyes to light up. "This treat…" It contained vacuum-sealed cannabis. Opening up another and another revealed much of the same.

"Wow!" Lynda marveled at the haul. "This place is loaded with pallets of the stuff."

"Tell me about it." Dex petted Barnabas behind his ear. "Good job, boy."

"There's cannabis edibles, THC vaping cartridges and psilocybin mushroom bars…" commented Agent Sylvester Ishikawa, his brown eyes wide with disbelief as he opened another pallet. At forty-two, the slender fifteen-year veteran of the DEA was Japanese and had short dark hair worn in an undercut that was slicked backward. "Looks like they made sure there was something for everyone."

"And now no one," quipped Dex, knowing that the illegal drugs would ultimately be destroyed. Barnabas barked, as if happy to take credit for his part.

"Yeah, that's the plan," Ishikawa agreed.

"We're all good with that," Lynda said in support. "The more we can separate the legal from illegal drugs, the better for everyone."

Dex couldn't agree more, having lost his only sister, Rita, years ago to a drug overdose, with heroin the deadly drug of choice. She'd never had a real chance to get cleaned up before being taken away before her time at the tender age of nineteen. He only wished he had been old enough to help her overcome the addiction and related poor choices she'd made in her life. With the better part of their job done, the team turned the cleanup work over to the Los Angeles County Sheriff's Department and its crime scene investigators. The DEA would continue to do its part in overturning every rock where illicit drugs and their facilitators were hiding. Dex intended to give Barnabas the rest of the day off, even while knowing that the job of taking on drug cartels and criminal gangs was never ending. Or so it seemed.

Two hours later, the agents had joined others in a conference room at the DEA's Los Angeles Division, which included within its jurisdiction Santa Ana and Ventura, California, Hawaii, Nevada and Guam. The special agent in charge was Rachel Zavatti, a tall and attractive fifty-year-old with hazel eyes and a chin-length gray shag. She had moved up the ladder in a hurry, thanks in large part to a successful takedown a decade ago of a notorious international cartel that was responsible for an illegal marijuana farm in the Midwest. Dex was admittedly impressed with her dedication to the job, which he shared in the absence of any meaningful relationship since ending things with his unfaithful girlfriend, Suzette, two years ago.

Right now, this was it for him and he was grateful for the opportunity to put his skills to good use.

"Job well done," Rachel said of their latest bust. "Apart from arresting a number of drug traffickers, including the reputed leader of the syndicate, Louis Johansson, we ended up confiscating roughly thirty pallets of vacuum-sealed cannabis, nearly four hundred pounds of cannabis edibles, thousands of THC vaping cartridges and over six hundred grams of psilocybin mushroom bars. I'd say that's quite a load for one operation."

"Not to mention the AR-15 semiautomatic assault rifles, .223 caliber assault rifles, some handguns and enough ammo to go to war," Dex pitched in, though doubtful this had slipped her mind, thorough as she was.

"Oh, did I fail to mention that?" she quipped good-naturedly. "Leave it up to Adair to cover all the bases."

"Next he'll be telling us he did it all by himself like a superhero," Lynda tossed out with a straight face.

"Or maybe just an average guy who displayed abilities Adair didn't even know he had," Ishikawa said. "Do we need to applaud him, or what?"

Dex chuckled, cool with being part of a team that learned not to take things too seriously, though at times it couldn't be helped. They all knew that when it came to the illicit drug trade and its negative impact on society, it was definitely no laughing matter. "I'd much rather give credit where credit's due," he offered modestly. "Barnabas found the marijuana without giving it a second thought. The K-9 knows his business and makes my job that much easier. If he were here and could do it, I'm sure he'd happily take a bow."

Rachel smiled. "I'm sure you deserve at least half the credit for his productivity. But Barnabas's half is still crucial to our operation." She smoothed creases on her open-front blazer. "In any event, before we start patting each other on the back, there are more important matters to discuss—" Dex noted a distinct change in her expression. She turned to a large presentation display and, using a remote, turned it on. A face appeared on the screen of an Asian female in her early thirties with short black hair in a wedge bob. "Last month, DEA Agent Roxanne Yamamoto was on an undercover operation on Kauai, Hawaii, when she died in an apparent single vehicle crash. What first seemed like an unfortunate accident has proven to be a deliberate act of murder. After a mechanical inspection of the vehicle, it was discovered that Agent Yamamoto's brake lines were cut, causing her to lose control of the car. Moreover, she was driving past midnight and didn't have her cell phone, which suggests that Roxanne was in a hurry to get away from one or more individuals. Both the phone and her laptop are missing, along with any pertinent information they contained, which we have thus far been unable to retrieve."

Dex winced at the sight of Roxanne Yamamoto on the screen. They were friends, hanging out together once after a drug bust in Las Vegas, in which seventy pounds of methamphetamine was seized, resulting in multiple arrests. Roxanne was a nice person who, like him, loved her work and gave her all. She didn't deserve to die, as it turned out, in the line of duty and at such a young age with her whole life still ahead of her.

Rachel switched to another picture. "This is the Maoli Lodge," she said. "It has long been suspected of being a front for drug trafficking with ties to the same crime organization that we busted wide-open today, but we haven't been able to make anything stick. Agent Yamamoto was working undercover there as a housekeeper, hoping to gather information that she could pass on to other agents in the field, as part of a Drug Task Force on drug-related criminality on Kauai that included members of the FBI and IRS, US Postal Inspectors and Kauai Police Department's vice section." Rachel's brow furrowed. "She was killed before Agent Yamamoto was able to tell us what, if anything, she had discovered with respect to criminal activity at the resort location. Though there is an active investigation by the locals into her death and suspicion that there may have been another vehicle involved in the crash, there are no solid leads at the moment as to any suspects." The special agent in charge sighed. "We need to find out what's going on at that lodge, if it's anything illegal, and who is responsible for the loss of one of our own."

She flipped to another image of a biracial male with brown eyes and a curly raven faux-hawk haircut. "Joseph Sizemore, age thirty-six, was the co-owner of the Maoli Lodge. He was being investigated as possibly being involved in the trafficking of drugs. Unfortunately, he died in a mysterious kayaking accident six months ago off the Nāpali Coast, effectively taking him out of the equation, though the probe of Sizemore's potential involvement is still ongoing." Rachel switched to another picture of an adult white female. "Katrina Sizemore is his thirty-two-year-old widow, who co-owned the lodge. Upon Sizemore's death, she took over as the sole owner. She's definitely a person of interest as someone who may be part of the illegal drug-trafficking operation."

Dex took in the image of the striking widow. She had big, bold, blue eyes and a square face with a dimpled chin. Long red hair was parted in the middle with voluminous curls. He imagined what a catch she was for her late husband. But was she also a drug trafficker, using her lodge as a legitimate means to funnel illegal profits?

"How's your piano playing talent these days, Adair?" Rachel got his attention.

Dex looked at her. He had learned to play the piano as a boy, taking lessons from his mother, who was an excellent pianist till the day she passed away five years ago. Though he hardly considered himself a great talent in that regard, Dex did feel he could more than hold his own when called upon to perform in a nonprofessional capacity. Indeed, he had played a few jazz numbers at the retirement party last year of fellow agent Bradley Lancaster. "I play every now and then," Dex said tentatively.

"Perfect." That seemed to be enough for her to consider him to be something akin to a concert pianist. "I need you to familiarize yourself with a few classic Hawaiian tunes."

"Uh, okay…" He cocked a brow, wondering where she was going with this.

"You'll be working undercover as a piano player at the Maoli Lodge," Rachel directed him. "They happen to be looking for a replacement for their pianist who is currently on maternity leave. Operating from the inside can give you a better opportunity to gather intelligence."

Undercover? Dex hesitated. Seriously? He had gone down this road before a time or two, and pulled it off masterfully. But not where it concerned using music in a covert operation. And what about Barnabas? Rachel clearly read his mind as she continued, "You'll be taking your K-9 with you. Fortunately, it's a pet friendly lodge, the perfect cover for Barnabas to see what shows up under his trusty radar. You need to pick up where Agent Yamamoto left off. Is that going to be a problem?"

"Not at all," Dex answered predictably. He could hardly turn down an assignment that apparently cost

Roxanne her life. And it would give him the opportunity to take stock of Katrina Sizemore up close and personal. "I'm sure Barnabas will welcome a trip to Hawaii and probably want to stay, once the dust settles."

"Not happening." The special agent in charge put her foot down. "He's much too valuable for us to give up anytime soon."

"Figured as much," he cracked. Not that he would ever even truly consider leaving his best friend behind. Unless, of course, they were able to retire to the island together, which also seemed very unlikely.

"You'll be Dex Matheson for the time being," she informed him, knowing that the cover would only work if it was difficult to prove otherwise. "With Agent Yamamoto's death, we need to be extra diligent in protecting your identity till we get what we need to complete the mission."

"Understood." Dex knew that she had borrowed the surname from Sally Matheson, her sister, who was a federal attorney.

"Good." Rachel turned her attention elsewhere. "Krause and Ishikawa, you'll be checking into the Maoli Lodge as Mr. and Mrs. Sylvester Hayashi to dig around for evidence of drug trafficking, while providing backup for Adair should all hell break loose."

"I always wanted to marry Ishikawa—or should I say, Hayashi—and have our honeymoon in Hawaii," Lynda joked.

"Your wish is my command, Mrs. Hayashi." Ishikawa played his part in earnest. "Of course, the job comes first."

"Absolutely!" she insisted in all seriousness.

"Glad we're clear on that." Rachel spoke in a commanding tone. "You'll be working with the Task Force investigating drug trafficking on the island and its connection to the lodge as well as to the crime syndicate right here in LA." She paused. "Any questions?" Dex decided that anything he had a problem with could be brought up later. Apparently, his colleagues felt the same way, prompting the special agent in charge to unceremoniously conclude, "So go pack your bags and let's get this done for Agent Yamamoto."

It was something Dex agreed wholeheartedly with. The worst thing would be for her death to be in vain. Especially if they could give Roxanne the ability to rest in peace. Half an hour later, fresh with the assignments handed out, Dex headed to his Huston Street Moorish style home in the Valley Village part of LA to prep Barnabas and brush up on his skills on the piano… Katrina Sizemore and her role, if any, in the trafficking of drugs and possibly the death of Agent Yamamoto squarely in his thoughts.

KATRINA SIZEMORE STOOD in slip-on espadrille flats at her ergonomic adjustable desk in the small office of the Maoli Lodge. It still blew her mind that she had fallen into the role of lodge owner all by her lonesome, following the untimely death six months ago of her husband, Joseph. Three years earlier, which seemed like a lifetime ago, they had relocated to Kauai from Salem, Oregon, with the dream of opening their own lodging accommodations on the amazing Hawaiian island where they had honeymooned four years prior to their move. They found the perfect place up for sale: a forty-room and four suites plantation-style oceanfront property on Poipu Road, with a swimming pool, its own tropical gardens, swaying coconut palm trees, mature monkeypod trees and spectacular mountain views. It was located in the neighborhood of Poipu, which in Hawaiian meant "crashing waves," on the south shore, a popular destination for tourists and locals. Neither of them realized just how much money it would take and how much work they would have to put in to run such a business successfully. Or the strain it would place on their marriage, which had begun to falter even before Joseph died in an accident while kayaking.

Katrina shuddered to think of what might have happened to them had he lived. Could things have continued to go the way they were without it costing them their marriage? Or the love they promised to hold on to forever, as if a bond that couldn't be broken? Were that the case, what would have happened to the lodge? Would either of them have been willing to give up what belonged to both of them with no hard feelings? She couldn't imagine remaining in business together while no longer husband and wife.

She ran thin fingers through her lengthy and loose crimson locks, feeling saddened and guilty that she had been left to make it work alone, thanks in part to a payout on Joseph's life insurance that helped keep the lodge afloat. But somehow she was determined to do just that, both in Joseph's memory and that of a housekeeper, Roxanne Kitaoka, who passed away last month in a car accident. Katrina still couldn't believe she was gone. Just like that. It still wasn't clear to her how this could happen. What was Roxanne doing out on the road past midnight? From what little Katrina knew of her life outside the lodge, in Roxanne's free time she seemed pretty much a homebody, similar to herself when not working, which for Katrina had proven to be a 24/7 job. When she did find the time, she ran, a favorite activity to keep in shape and take in as much of the wondrous landscape as possible. The authorities had been sketchy at best in telling her anything, but indicated that Roxanne's death had been the result of foul play. Who would have wanted her dead? And why?

As she pondered these disturbing thoughts, Katrina did miss her employee, who even if they weren't friends, was like family as part of the staff, and could only hope that Roxanne didn't suffer too much at the end, while praying the same as well for Joseph. When she heard her name called, it startled Katrina. Looking up from her musing, she saw Alyson Tennison, her assistant manager, standing there. Six years Katrina's senior, at thirty-eight, Alyson was just as slender and maybe an inch shorter than Katrina's five feet eight inches height. An attractive blue-eyed divorcée, she came with lots of experience in hotel management and seemed a perfect fit for the position.

"Aloha." Katrina spoke routinely.

"Didn't mean to wake you up," Alyson quipped, sporting a mid-length brunette blunt lob.

"I'm wide-awake. My mind was just wandering." Katrina colored. "What's up?"

"There's a gentleman here to see you."

"Oh…?" Katrina wondered if it was the new landscaper checking in. Or someone else hoping to sell her on this or that for the lodge, now that this role had fallen entirely on her shoulders as the sole proprietor.

"He's applying for the pianist opening," Alyson said. "I figured the best way to check him out was to audition. You'll find him waiting in the lounge at the piano."

"Good idea." Katrina smiled. With her rather hectic life these days, she had practically forgotten about needing a piano player. Since her current pianist, Gina Oxenberg, was on maternity leave, they had substituted her impressive skills with taped music, mostly Hawaiian, along with some jazz and easy listening. Maybe they could get by without hiring someone for the job. *Might as well at least see what he brings to the table*, Katrina told herself. She glanced at her casual attire of a gold scoop-neck top and black straight-leg trousers. Deciding they were acceptable for greeting a prospective employee, she followed Alyson out of the office.

They split up in the lobby that had pearl mosaic tiles for the flooring and Hawaiian-style furnishings and tropical plants. Katrina could hear the baby grand piano as she stepped inside the Kahiko Lounge, which was decorated in 1940s retro élan. She spied the handsome man seated at the piano. African American and in his early thirties, she guessed; he was tall, muscled, with short jet-black hair in a line up haircut and a five-o'clock shadow beard. He wore a floral print shirt and brown slacks. She noticed that a gorgeous golden retriever was seated by his side on the floor, seemingly just as enchanted by the piano sounds of the Hawaiian song, "King's Serenade," as she was.

When he noticed her standing there, the piano player stopped on a dime and faced her. Katrina could see that he was even better looking upon gazing into incredibly deep sable-gray eyes. Trying to find words in that moment, she managed to utter, "That was lovely."

He flashed a brilliant smile, making her weak in the knees. "Thanks."

"I take it you're here for the job…?" Katrina gave him a knowing look.

"Yeah, if it's still available." A long arm stretched

out and his large hand reached for a shake. "I'm Dex Matheson."

She cupped hands with him, feeling as though her own were engulfed within his. "Aloha. Katrina Sizemore. And, yes, it's still available," she admitted, finding herself wanting to hear more of his piano playing. She wondered where he learned the craft and was even more curious about other aspects of his life that made the man before her.

"Cool." Dex grinned again, displaying white teeth, straight as an arrow. He gazed down at the dog that now stood on its four legs. "This is Barnabas."

"Hi, Barnabas." She petted him on the base of his neck. The dog licked her hand, seeming to take to her instantly. Good sign? Looking back at its owner, Katrina remembered there was still a process to go through before she could hire him. She had been burned before in bringing on someone who couldn't or refused to measure up to the job. Something told her Dex would measure up just fine. But still... "Why don't we head to my office and get your basic information and I'll tell you what we're looking for in a piano player."

Dex gave her an agreeable and confident nod. "Works for me."

Katrina smiled and led the way.

Chapter Two

Dex was admittedly transfixed by the red-haired beauty of Katrina Sizemore. The screen image of the lodge owner, nice as it was, did no justice when compared to the real person. The face, taut and squared, was flawless and he loved that cute little cleft on her chin. And could those enticing eyes be any bluer, as if taken straight from the ocean itself on a good day? He was also taken by her slender physique and just the right height in relation to his own size. Under other circumstances, Dex imagined they would be a good—and maybe perfect—fit. But at the moment, he feared that beneath the very appealing facade could well be someone involved in the world of illegal drugs. Worse yet was that the widow may have also played a role in the murder of his fellow DEA agent Roxanne Yamamoto.

But Dex took a proverbial step back, even as he sat in the cranberry tub chair, not wanting to get ahead of himself just yet as he did what he needed to do to convince Katrina Sizemore to hire him as a piano player. Having left Barnabas by the piano with his leash attached to it, Dex quickly scanned the office, with a picture window looking out onto an impressive botanical garden and sand-colored vinyl flooring. There were two desks with laptops, a two-drawer white lateral file cabinet, a printer on a folding table and a ceiling fan. A closed door presumably was a storage closet. Or could it lead to another room?

Turning back to the proprietor as she took a seat in the chair angled toward his, Dex gave her a believable friendly grin. "This is a really nice place you have here."

"Mahalo." She clasped her hands thoughtfully and he noted the wedding band on her finger. It indicated to him that she was having trouble letting go, as he would have, had he lost the love of his life prematurely.

This gave Dex an opening. "How long have you and your husband owned it?" He played the innocent.

"Three years." She eyed the ring self-consciously, then unclasped her hands. "I lost my husband six months ago," she murmured.

"I'm sorry to hear that," Dex told her sincerely, even though already privy to this information.

"He died in a kayaking accident." Her shoulders slumped. "So, I'm afraid it's just me now."

"You must have your hands full going it alone?" He wondered if that sounded more coldhearted than he'd intended. Worse would be if it came across as a come-on. Even if the appeal was there, and it was, he had no interest in going after the widow like a lovestruck teenager. She was likely still in love with her late husband. "What I meant was that I could only imagine the burden of running a lodge in Poipu, where tourists flock, with its various attractions," Dex sought to clarify.

"It's fine," she said evenly, not appearing to pick up on his probing. "You're right, it has been over-whelming at times. But I'm hanging in there, thanks in large part to the support of my staff and being fortunate enough to own a lodge in the heart of Poipu, keeping me busy."

If she was guilty of anything criminal, Dex was not picking up on it at present. He wondered if his attraction to the beautiful widow might have something to do with that. Or could she really be blameless in the suspected drug activity at the lodge that had apparently cost Roxanne her life?

"So, tell me a little about yourself, Mr. Matheson," Dex heard the soft voice, breaking away from his reverie as he locked eyes with the proprietor.

Don't blow this, he thought, as if she could somehow see right through him. "For starters, please call me Dex," he insisted, if for no other reason than it was easier to keep from slipping up if he kept the moniker to himself. But, better still, he preferred the more personal first name communication for building trust and getting information.

She smiled. "Dex it is. And please call me Katrina."

"Okay." He nodded agreeably. "Well, Katrina, I just moved here after living the last few years in the Los Angeles area."

"Why Hawaii?" came the expected question. "And Kauai, in particular, if you don't mind my asking?"

"Not at all," Dex said smoothly. Especially when he had his own questions for her, when the time was right. "I was at a time in my life when I felt I needed a change. I'd visited the Islands while in college and found Kauai the most to my liking. When an opportunity presented itself, I decided to go give island life a try."

She raised a thin brow curiously. "You mean an opportunity other than playing piano at a lodge?"

He chuckled. "Yeah, you could say that. A friend of mine has a local private investigation agency and asked if I'd be willing to work there part-time as a PI. Nothing too heavy," Dex stressed, "missing spouses, cheating spouses, rescuing cats from trees. Stuff like that. Since I worked as a private detective in LA before I got injured and decided I'd saved enough to go into an early semi-retirement, I figured, why not?" *Hope she buys this without needing to embellish the story too much more*, he thought.

"Makes sense to me." She laughed a little, then regarded him keenly. "Must have been a serious injury?"

"I hurt my back while chasing a stalker." This

much was true. At least hurting the back part. Only it happened during a major drug bust in Santa Ana two years ago. Though he recovered fully, he still felt a twinge in his lower back every now and then. "Not a big deal. Good excuse to move to paradise, anyhow," he kidded.

"If you say so." She studied him. "Did you move here with family or…"

"Just me," he told her without preface. He wondered if her interest was purely out of curiosity. Or her way of asking if he was single and available? Did it matter? She was off-limits, romantically speaking, as a suspect while on an undercover mission.

"I see." Katrina brushed her dainty little nose. "How long have you been playing the piano, Dex?"

"Since I was knee-high. Learned from my mother, who wanted to make sure she passed the talent along to me and my sister, Rita."

"That's nice. Your mother was obviously successful in her efforts."

Dex grinned. "Yeah, I'm happy about that." He only wished Rita hadn't blown it in losing sight of everything she had to offer to the world before it was too late to turn things around.

Katrina leaned forward, making Dex fight the urge to stretch out his long arm and touch her attractive face. "Well, the job doesn't pay particularly well, but does require a couple of hours of your time five evenings a week and two afternoons. Moreover, as my regular piano player may or may not return once her maternity leave ends, it might only be a temporary gig." She paused. "Does this still sound like something you would be interested in?"

She was giving him a way out of this, as if to undercut her own need for a pianist. Was this an attempt to play it safe as a drug trafficker who had second thoughts about having someone new around? He waited a long beat, pretending to be reconsidering whether he wanted to take the position, before eyeing her directly and responding coolly, "Yes, definitely. As I alluded to, I'm in pretty good shape financially, so pay whatever you like. I enjoy playing the piano and entertaining folks with a blend of Hawaiian, contemporary, easy listening and soul music. I'll gladly work whatever hours and days you need me until your regular piano player returns."

"Hard to argue with that." Katrina's full lips curved upward at the corners. "I guess that settles it. You're hired."

Dex flashed his teeth. "Great."

"I'll just need to verify you're with the private investigation agency you indicated you'll be working for on Kauai…"

Smart of you to ask, Dex mused. "Of course." He gave her the cell phone number of the agency and the contact there, Glenn Nakao, who had worked with the DEA in the past and been briefed in advance, agreeing to play along. Being a real detective firm that could easily be looked up on the internet would solidify Dex's cover that much more.

Katrina seemed satisfied with the ease of his co-operation. "When can you start?" she asked eagerly.

Not wishing to appear overeager himself, while at the same time needing to ingratiate himself into her world as soon as possible to get some answers, he replied evenly, "Whenever you like."

"Tomorrow at noon would be great," Katrina said promptly. "We tend to get many of our guests around that time on a Wednesday. It would be wonderful to welcome them with a drink and some entertaining piano music."

"Tomorrow it is." Dex kept his tone relaxed and sure. It would give him some extra time to acclimate himself to the surroundings and size up the lady herself.

"Perfect." She offered him a pleased smile and got to her feet. "Why don't I give you a quick tour and introduce you to the staff."

"Sounds good to me." The more people he met, the better the chances to get a read on them and assess if any or all could be involved in illicit drug activity and murder.

"ALOHA AND WELCOME to the Maoli Lodge," Katrina greeted the new arrivals, who had been introduced to her as Sylvester and Lynda Hayashi and were wearing floral leis.

"Aloha," they returned in unison. "Happy to be able to spend some quality time at your fabulous lodge," Lynda voiced enthusiastically.

Katrina smiled. "If you need anything, just let me or a member of the staff know," she told them.

"We will," Sylvester promised, and gave a friendly nod to Dex, before the couple went on their way.

"Looks like the guests are already feeling right at home," Dex remarked.

"That's the whole idea," Katrina uttered, knowing it was what she and Joseph had envisioned from the start. Even if he was no longer there to share the experience, she knew it was all about providing a welcoming atmosphere for visitors, who would hopefully come back again and again.

"It's working," he declared, making her wonder if Dex was referring to himself as well.

Katrina continued to show her new hire around, surprising herself in already starting to feel somewhat close to him, if that was possible. She sensed she could trust Dex, though she had yet to even check out his reference. With his ID seemingly legit, this was likely only a mere formality and nothing to worry about. She admitted that there was something mysteriously enticing about the piano player that attracted her, even beyond his handsome features. Would she get to know him more? Or was that asking for trouble, considering she wasn't in the market right now for romance. Was he?

She introduced him to Alyson, her assistant manager. "Nice to meet you formally," Alyson said, after they had exchanged words earlier.

"You too," Dex said.

"Can't wait to hear more of your piano playing."

He grinned. "I'll try not to disappoint."

For whatever reason, Katrina felt a spasm of jealousy, which she had no right to. Alyson was a natural flirt and Dex had admitted, essentially, to being a single man and was presumably available to the right woman. Maybe that was her assistant manager, who was divorced and looking for love again. She generally didn't encourage workplace romance. But Dex was a part-time employee and would likely move on once Gina returned, and Katrina had no desire to try and dictate his or anyone else's love life. Especially when her own love life was nonexistent these days and had already hit the skids in her marriage before Joseph's death, whether she wanted to face up to it or not.

They finished the tour back where they'd started in the Kahiko Lounge. Katrina introduced Dex to her bartender, Gordon Guerrero. The thickly built, forty-year-old half Hawaiian had a black-blond Caesar crop top short hairstyle, a short black boxed beard and large brown eyes. "Aloha," Gordon said tonelessly, as they shook hands.

"Aloha," Dex said back, not seeming at all intimidated by the bulkier bartender. Not that he had reason to be, as Katrina felt Gordon was actually a teddy bear in spite of his hardened demeanor.

"Dex is our new pianist," Katrina told him.

"What about Gina?" Gordon threw out worriedly. Their piano player was married to his cousin, Marciel.

"When she's ready to return, she has a job waiting for her," Katrina promised.

This seemed to ease his concerns and Gordon said, "I'd best get back to work now."

"Is he always that friendly?" Dex asked as they walked away from him and toward the piano.

"Yes, pretty much." Katrina chuckled. "Seriously, Gordon's a good guy, if a little rough around the edges." He had never given them any trouble and had actually become friends with Joseph, even doing things away from the lodge, such as deep sea fishing together.

"I'll take your word for that." Dex's voice was laced with sarcasm, but he seemed able to adjust easily enough to each different personality he encountered amongst the staff.

Dex's dog, Barnabas, sat quietly beside the piano. Katrina loved domesticated animals and would have one or more of her own, had the demands of running a lodge not been too much to properly care for a pet.

"Have you been a good boy?" Dex asked, untangling the leash from the piano leg. He petted the dog, who reacted favorably, clearly smitten with his owner. "Yeah, I think you have."

Katrina imagined that the two were inseparable, other than when Dex was doing private investigation work. Barnabas stood and sniffed her hand playfully. She giggled. "I like you too."

Dex seemed glad to hear that by his agreeable

expression. "I better take him home and get out of your hair."

"Okay." She almost hated to see them leave, as though Katrina would never lay eyes on the man and his dog again. Which was silly, of course. After all, Dex was the new piano player. Meaning that Barnabas would also likely make a return visit. "See you tomorrow at noon."

"On the nose," he assured her, and their shoulders brushed, sending electricity throughout Katrina's body. Had Dex noticed too? Or could the whole thing have been her overactive imagination?

Katrina watched as they headed for the door and the humidity and sunshine that awaited them outside, before she went on her merry way. Even then, for whatever reason, she had the feeling she was being observed. Which was odd, considering that she was inside and saw only a few people wandering about seemingly caught up in their own worlds. That included the new guests, Sylvester and Lynda Hayashi, who were busy studying a brochure as if it held the secrets to the universe. Was she really being surveilled? If so, by whom? And for what reason? Or was that, too, only in her head?

Katrina chewed on those uneasy thoughts as she headed back to her office to verify the identity and work reference of Dex Matheson.

DEX STILL HAD Katrina Sizemore very much on his mind as he loaded Barnabas into his rented dark gray Ford Expedition XLT, then hopped behind the wheel. Her striking features notwithstanding, was the lodge owner hiding something relevant to their investigation? It was up to him to find out, whatever it took, with the help of undercover agents Krause and Ishikawa. Along with, of course, his trusty companion who was making himself comfortable beside Dex. He started up the vehicle and drove around the property, looking for entrances and exits that might be employed by traffickers, along with angles and out-of-the-way places and spaces that could provide cover or hideaways for drug activity. There was a black Ford Transit full-size cargo van parked out back that could possibly be used for transporting illicit drugs. What had Roxanne uncovered that likely cost the DEA agent her life?

Knowing he had time to make some determinations with his new piano gig, Dex left the lodge grounds and headed down Poipu Road en route to the rented cottage he would be calling home during his stay on Kauai. It was the same place Roxanne had operated from before she was killed. He soon reached his destination on Nakoa Street in the nearby unincorporated community of Koloa, but far enough away so as not to draw attention from the locals. Leaving the car, he let Barnabas out and they headed to their new temporary home away from home.

The one-story, two-bedroom farmhouse-style residence had merbau hardwood flooring and vaulted ceilings, with large picture windows covered by

fabric blinds. A spacious kitchen had slate countertops and stainless steel appliances as part of an
open concept architecture, with modest contemporary furnishings. As Barnabas sized up the place,
Dex walked through while imagining Roxanne being
made and having to make a hasty escape for her
life. It had been scoured for DNA, fingerprints and
other evidence, but nothing had stuck with respect
to clues as to her killer. Dex couldn't help but think
they may have missed something crucial toward getting some answers.

He peeked through the blinds and saw a covered
lanai that overlooked a fully fenced backyard with
fruit trees and plenty of room for Barnabas to play
and get some exercise. Dex let the dog out the back
door. "Stay out of trouble," he teased him. After un-
loading his things from the car, Dex went back inside and plotted his strategy for learning more from
and about Katrina, even while the better part of him
was just as interested in getting to know the lady
herself. Or was that a dumb idea? Maybe not, as he
sensed her assessing him with more than a passing
glance. If she had no dirty laundry in the closet, who
knew if something could be there waiting for them
both to explore.

Just as he contemplated that tantalizing thought,
Dex heard the sound of a vehicle pulling up to the
cottage. He looked out the front window and saw a
blue Hyundai Elantra GT in the driveway. Lynda
and Ishikawa got out and approached the house. Dex

opened the door and greeted them teasingly, "I was beginning to think that you were too caught up in your honeymoon, Mr. and Mrs. Hayashi, to break away from the Maoli Lodge."

"Yeah, right." Lynda rolled her green eyes. "This coming from the man who couldn't seem to take his eyes off the lovely widow."

Dex didn't deny it, but countered with a more defensive tone than he'd intended. "If I'm not mistaken, it's what I've been tasked with."

"Such a grueling task, Adair," she quipped, "but someone's got to do it, right?"

"That's why I get the big bucks." He went along with the ribbing, while knowing that in reality being a DEA special agent was anything but a get rich scheme. But it did give him a general sense of satisfaction that could never be measured in dollars and cents. Something he was sure motivated his colleagues as well.

"We've all got a job to do," Ishikawa said forthrightly, moving past him and into the cottage. Dex allowed Lynda to follow and he went in afterward. "I take it you were hired?"

Dex nodded. "I start in earnest tomorrow at noon."

"Good. Hope you can pull it off with your piano skills without arousing suspicion."

"I'm sure I'll be able to hold my own," Dex assured him, "while seeing what I can dig up."

"Never had a doubt." Ishikawa patted him on the

shoulder and looked around. "So, where's your side-kick?"

"Out back. There's lots of space for Barnabas to run around without getting lost, till he's called upon in the line of duty."

"Good for him."

Dex eyed Lynda, who had taken out her cell phone to check for messages. "Come up with anything yet on your end?"

"Still in the honeymoon phase," Ishikawa replied, metaphorically speaking. "We'll be scoping out the lodge in the coming days and seeing what we can learn about its possible ties to drug trafficking."

"I studied the grounds and can see some possi-bilities for trafficking drugs in and out," Dex said. "Barnabas and I will look into it."

"Good. Maybe we can nip this thing in the bud sooner than later."

Dex gazed at Lynda, who was still glued to her phone. "Care to let us in on who or what's got your attention?"

"Sorry." She cut the phone off. "That was Mar-tin," she said apologetically. Lynda was currently dating Martin O'Sullivan, an investigator for LA County Sheriff's Narcotic Bureau, who was part of the downtown drug bust. "According to him, drug kingpin Louis Johansson is already starting to talk."

"Didn't take much to get him to look out for num-ber one," Dex stated, sure that Johansson was trying to cut a deal to save his own neck. He was also certain that the trafficker couldn't be trusted as far as you could throw him. Dex was confident this would be a factor in seeing what they could get from him and what it was worth, if anything.

"Never does when the screws start to tighten," Ishikawa remarked flippantly, scratching his jaw.

"Martin believes that the ties between the trafficking of drugs in Southern California and Hawaii—Kauai, in particular—may run deeper than we think. So it's even more important that we make the case with the Maoli Lodge as a possible vector for illegal drugs and the related murder of Agent Yamamoto."

Dex furrowed his brow. "I hear you," he muttered. "We'll do what we need to and find out if there's a case to be made. And, if so, how deep it runs." He considered that Katrina could be nothing more than an innocent pawn in a complicated scheme. Or deceptively attractive on the outside, but inside guilty as sin of one or more serious offenses, including responsibility for the death of a federal agent.

"So, this is where Agent Yamamoto laid her head when away from the lodge?" Lynda peeked into the master bedroom. "It's almost as though she's speaking to us from the grave."

"You mean like a ghost?" Ishikawa's mouth hung open.

"Like someone who had unfinished business and can't rest till it's done."

Dex put more weight on one leg than the other.

"Can't say I believe in the supernatural," he had to admit. "But I do believe in justice being served when crimes are committed. And since Roxanne was my friend, I'm definitely keen on doing right by her. If that means speaking back to Agent Yamamoto, as such, while caught in spiritual unrest, so be it." To be successful in this endeavor, he sensed that they would need Katrina's cooperation, voluntary or not.

Chapter Three

The following day, Katrina was still rattled by a feeling of being spied upon as she sipped passion fruit tea in the loft suite she called home and her safety net. Claiming the largest of the four suites when she and Joseph bought the lodge, it had three bedrooms, tigerwood exotic flooring and bamboo ceiling fans throughout, and a tropical-style kitchen with smoky quartz countertops, a distressed oak kitchen island and farmhouse apron front sink. The floor-to-ceiling windows in the great room offered plenty of natural light, with plantation shutters. She marveled at the carefully selected custom-made furnishings, an eclectic mixture of woven seagrass and rattan pieces, accented with areca palm and bird-of-paradise plants. While it created a warm and cozy atmosphere, Katrina knew this could not compensate for the loneliness that had started to set in. But when did it truly began? Was it after she had lost her husband? Or before? Would that all-important sense of completion and being loved ever return? Or had it ever been there in the first place during her marriage?

Exactly what am I trying to say? she questioned, while standing barefoot and still in her short satin chemise nightgown. That Joseph never truly loved her? She rejected this, believing that he did in his own way. And her love for him was real too. She just wasn't sure that what they had together was everything she'd signed up for when marrying him and relocating to Kauai. Whether that was widow's remorse or something more, Katrina tried to put it out of her mind as she watched a gecko crawl up the wall before she headed into the master bedroom. It was spacious with wicker furniture, a private lanai and an en suite bath that included a jetted tub.

She got dressed, tied her hair into a side ponytail, and was ready to begin her morning chores and responsibilities. Afterward, she looked forward to listening to Dex work his magic at the piano, believing he was more than capable of delivering for their guests for as long as Gina was away.

When Katrina stepped inside her office, with plans to go over the budget, work schedules and other items that commanded her attention as owner of the lodge, she couldn't help but notice the folded piece of paper sitting on her desk. She picked it up curiously and unfolded it, reading the message. It was sloppily written, as though the writer was in a hurry, but still legible.

Don't believe what you've been told about your husband's death. No accident. He was murdered. Watch your back.

Katrina dropped the note on the desk as though it were on fire, and put a hand to her mouth in shock. She looked about the office as if expecting to find whoever left the note. But it was empty aside from her. Gazing back at the piece of paper, she felt compelled to read it again, as though her eyes had played a cruel trick on her. Picking it up, she read it again and saw the same disturbing words. Who would play such a cruel joke on her? And why? Was it possible that Joseph's death was not from the kayaking accident after all, but had only been masked by it? If so, why would anyone wish to harm her husband, much less kill him?

A hand on her shoulder nearly made Katrina jump out of her skin. She jerked around in a defensive manner, sure that she was about to be attacked, but saw that it was Alyson standing there. "Hey, are you okay?" she asked innocuously enough.

"Yes. You startled me, that's all," Katrina responded honestly.

"Sorry. I saw you standing there, looking as though you'd been spooked by something." Alyson twisted her lips regretfully. "Guess I only made things worse."

"You didn't." Katrina sighed and looked at the

paper she was still holding. "But you're right, I was spooked...by this—" She passed the note to her.

Alyson stared at it, her face coloring almost instantly. "Where did you get this?"

"It was on my desk when I came in." Katrina gazed at her. "Did you see anyone in here?"

"No. Not when I was last in the office, about fifteen minutes ago."

"So someone must have dropped it off between then and now?" Katrina surmised disconcertingly, believing that she would likely have noticed since Alyson had to pass by her desk to get to her own.

"I'll ask the staff if anyone saw someone come this way," she said. "Or leave."

Katrina nodded, all types of thoughts running through her head. It was difficult enough just trying to come to terms with Joseph dying in a kayaking accident. Now someone was indicating otherwise. What was she to believe? "What do you make of this?" Katrina asked, valuing her opinion.

For once, Alyson seemed at a loss for words. "Maybe someone's idea of a sick joke?" she finally suggested.

It was Katrina's first reaction too. But it didn't make sense. "What would anyone have to gain by joking about my husband's death?" she questioned. "To watch me become unglued just for the sake of it?"

"You're right." Alyson handed the note back to her. "There's got to be more to it." She paused.

"Do you think Joseph really could have been murdered…?"

Katrina considered this for a long beat, trying to picture that horrifying possibility and what implications arose from it, before answering candidly, "I don't know." She placed the note inside the pocket of her knit pants and said determinedly, "But I need to find out."

DEX MADE HIMSELF comfortable at the piano as Barnabas sat beside him, curiously observing those who were present in the Kahiko Lounge drinking, talking or waiting to hear music. *I've got this*, Dex thought, confident in his ability to draw on his musical roots and skills to perform in an undercover role. He noted that Katrina was standing near the entrance, her gaze fixed on him. Was it his imagination or did she seem troubled? Maybe she was suspicious with his hastily arranged reference. Worse, perhaps she was having second thoughts about his ability to hold the attention of his audience as part of their experience at the lodge.

Guess I'll find out soon enough, he told himself. He started off with a classic Hawaiian song, "Ke Kali Nei Au." That was followed by a string of country, soul, easy listening, and more Hawaiian songs he had learned to play. The audience seemed receptive enough. All, that was, but Katrina, who looked as though she would rather be somewhere else. He couldn't help but wonder if there were other things on her mind. Such as drug trafficking and laundering of money through a legitimate business. Instinctively, Dex pushed back from the latter thoughts, sensing something else was weighing heavily based on her facial expressions.

During a break, he walked up to the lodge owner, unsure what to expect, and said, "Everything okay?"

"I'd like to hire you," Katrina responded straight-forwardly.

Dex cocked a brow. "I thought you already had employed my services?"

"As a private investigator," she made clear.

Admittedly, he hadn't seen that coming. Dex tried to imagine what she would need investigated. Actually, he could think of a few things. Perhaps she was trying to get ahead of whatever may be coming down with the probe into possible illegal activity at the lodge. Beginning to feel the heat from living a double life and looking for a way out? Or was there more going on with her than met the eye?

"Why do you want a PI?" he asked, curious while keeping an open mind.

Katrina looked around nervously and back, before responding ambiguously, "Can we talk in my office?"

"Sure." Dex attached Barnabas's leash to the piano leg wanting him to stay put, then followed her out of the lounge, through the lobby and into the office where he'd been hired. Only this time things seemed much more tense. "What's going on?" he asked, peering into her lovely but clearly disturbed face.

Katrina took a piece of paper out of her pocket and handed it to him. "This was waiting for me on my desk this morning," she uttered.

He read it.

Don't believe what you've been told about your husband's death. No accident. He was murdered. Watch your back.

Dex recalled that Rachel Zavatti, the special agent in charge, had noted that Joseph Sizemore was killed when his kayak capsized. It was thought to be an accidental drowning, but remained suspicious, considering that he had been under investigation for using the lodge to traffic illicit drugs. Did someone have solid information to prove foul play was involved? Dex eyed Sizemore's widow, who seemed genuine in her belief that his death was an accident. "Do you know who left the note?"

"I have no idea," Katrina insisted. "Alyson is asking around to see if any of the staff saw someone heading to or away from my office this morning."

"What do you know about your husband's death?" Dex asked, making sure his tone wasn't accusatory.

"Only what I was told—that it was an accident." She sucked in a steadying breath. "Joseph loved to go kayaking. He and a friend went out that day and apparently got caught in a shore break wave before they got very far, causing the kayak to overturn. Joseph went under and didn't survive. It was investigated and concluded that his death was, in fact, accidental. I accepted that. But now I get this cryptic message signifying otherwise and I'm just not sure what to believe."

Dex shared her concern with the note and wanted to dig deeper to see if it was a hoax. Or if someone knew something worth pursuing about the nature of Sizemore's death. If he was murdered, was it in relation to the Drug Task Force and DEA's investigation of drug trafficking on the island? And what, if anything, might Katrina know about it? Dex zeroed in on the "Watch your back" part of the message. Was this a veiled threat against her?

"I'd be happy to look into this," Dex told Katrina, in keeping with his undercover role as a private investigator. "There may be nothing to it. Or it could be that your husband's death was no accident, as reported. Did he have any enemies that you know of?"

She shook her head adamantly. "No. Joseph wasn't the type to make enemies. Quite the opposite. It's just that…" Her eyes shifted uncomfortably. "Last month, one of my housekeepers, Roxanne Kitaoka, was killed in a car accident on Kaumualii Highway. The police say she was murdered, but have never explained the circumstances. Now I'm wondering if somehow there could be a link between her death and Joseph's."

Dex had been wondering the same ever since

being given the assignment, in spite of the official cause of Sizemore's death being listed as accidental. Now there was even more reason to be suspicious, especially considering Roxanne's own undercover investigation at the Maoli Lodge. Dex kept his cool while resisting the desire to come clean with Katrina, who was still technically a suspect in the drug-trafficking probe, even if he was beginning to believe her hands were clean. "That is something worth looking into," he told her levelly. "You just need to be prepared for whatever I may find..."

She nodded, ill at ease. "I just need to know, one way or the other."

So do I, Dex mused, especially where it concerned her. The last thing he wanted was for the alluring lodge owner to be up to her neck in criminal activities. His gut told him this wasn't the case and he could usually trust his instincts. But could the same be said for her late husband? Was Joseph Sizemore running a drug-trafficking operation right under his wife's pretty nose? Either way, Dex intended to use this new opening to further his investigation at the lodge. "Okay, I'll do some digging, starting with who may have left the note. Mind if I hang on to it?"

"Please do, if it can help you track down whoever wrote it."

Dex deposited it in the pocket of his chino pants. He doubted that whoever had left it would also leave fingerprints or DNA that hadn't already been corrupted, but it was worth a shot. "What's the friend's name who was with your husband on the kayaking trip?"

"Larry Nakanishi. He runs a water sports and gear shop in Lihue."

Dex took out his cell phone and entered the information. "I'll need to speak with your staff to see if anyone knows anything about the message." He left off for now any possibility that someone she was employing could be involved in her husband's death.

"I understand." Katrina met his eyes. "Do I need to pay for your services in advance or…?"

"That won't be necessary," he explained. "Just poking around a bit won't cost you anything. If I learn something useful, we can discuss payment then." Truthfully, he wasn't interested in taking her money for something he needed to do for his own investigation. But he wasn't exactly at liberty to reveal his mission to her just yet.

"Mahalo." Somehow, she managed a smile through the worry lines that sat softly on her forehead. "There's one other thing…" Her voice shook. "Lately, I've had a strange feeling that someone has been watching me."

"Really?" Dex jutted his chin thoughtfully. "I take it this feeling started before you found the note?"

"Yes. I've wanted to believe it was all in my head," Katrina confessed. "But now I'm not so sure. Especially after that unsettling message…and the warning to watch my back. I don't know if I should be scared or not."

Dex wanted to say *not*, but when piecing together what he knew and still needed to uncover, giving her a false sense of security would not be a smart move, all things considered. But having her afraid of her own shadow at this point was not the way to go either. "My advice is for you to not read too much into the feeling of being watched. At least not until you have a bit more to go on in that regard. Could be that between your husband's death and the housekeeper's, it's found a way to play on your psyche."

"You're probably right," she relented, her voice elevating. "I'll try not to get spooked by what's been an invisible presence, more or less."

"Good idea." Dex still didn't want to leave it at that. "Nevertheless, keep your eyes open," he warned, "and don't let your guard down as it relates to being aware of your surroundings, even at the lodge."

Katrina smiled. "I'll try not to."

Her smile accentuated her good looks, and he returned it, welcoming seeing her like that. "In the meantime, I'll try to track down whoever sent the note and go from there. In the meantime, if you receive any more messages, let me know."

She nodded. "I will."

"Well, I better get back to the lounge," he said reluctantly. "I have one more set on the piano."

"Go," she told him. "I can see that everyone is enjoying you playing, myself included. I'll be fine."

"Okay." Dex found himself wanting to spend

more time with her outside of an official capacity. But blowing his cover might not be a smart idea. Certainly not if they wanted to continue unimpeded in completing an investigation Roxanne began. He was about to leave when he noticed that a ringlet of hair had managed to escape Katrina's long ponytail and fall across her brow. Without giving it a thought, Dex raised his hand and touched her soft skin, feeling a jolt in return. Had she felt it, too, as he tucked the errant strand behind her ear? "There, that's better," he said equably.

She blushed. "Thanks for noticing."

"My pleasure." He grinned and their eyes locked for a long moment of a connection, before Dex did the only sensible thing he could at that point. He walked away while he was still able to.

Chapter Four

Dex showed Lynda Krause and Sylvester Ishikawa the note someone had left for Katrina, as he huddled with the undercover DEA agents in their room at the lodge that was furnished with two queen beds. Having placed the piece of paper in a plastic bag to try and preserve evidence, should it come to that, Dex said troublingly, "Sizemore's death may not have been accidental..."

Lynda studied the note. "Hmm... Could this have come from someone who's simply venting because he or she doesn't agree with the medical examiner's findings?"

"Maybe," he had to allow, knowing that the note was hardly proof of a homicide in and of itself. "But were that the case, why not simply tell Katrina face-to-face that you believe someone murdered her late husband? Why the scare tactics and anonymity?"

"Point taken. It would also tie into the theory that Sizemore may have been involved in drug trafficking and bit off more than he could chew."

"Yeah, he could easily have gotten in way over his head," Ishikawa pitched in, "and was put out to pasture when he wanted out. Or his usefulness to those calling the shots was up."

"Both those angles are realistic possibilities." Dex didn't discount the ways traffickers could take out someone they wanted dead. "We have to see if this mystery messenger knows what he or she is talking about. I'd like to get the note dusted for any usable prints, analyzed for DNA, etc."

"Can't hurt to try," Ishikawa contended, grabbing the bag. "Even if it's probably a long shot."

"Yeah," Dex agreed. "It's a start anyway. Whoever left the message obviously wanted to get Katrina's attention. We need to know why and if this is connected to our overall investigation in any way."

"It is now," Lynda declared. "And maybe that was the point, to help her to connect the dots—assuming she wasn't already in on the blueprint."

"Katrina hired me as a private investigator," Dex informed them.

"Is that right?" Ishikawa's eyes widened.

"That note freaked her out. She wants to know who sent it and if there's any merit to the claim that her husband was murdered."

"Smart move on her part," Lynda said. "I'd want to know too, considering."

"Looks like having that second undercover PI role was the right move," Ishikawa stated. "It will allow you to operate more in plain view without fear of blowing your other cover."

"Yeah, I was thinking the same thing." Dex leaned against the wall. He would still work with Barnabas, too, when he could and it was necessary. As for Katrina, she may or may not have legitimate concerns. She deserved to know the truth about her husband, regardless of whatever he may have been up to. "I'm going to nose around and see what I can find out. If Sizemore was murdered, to go along with Roxanne's death, that could very well put Katrina in danger too."

"I don't disagree." Lynda wrinkled her nose. "Everything is still on the table at this point."

"We'll stay on the drug-trafficking angle," Ishikawa said, "and see if we can come up with whatever Agent Yamamoto had latched on to."

"Good." Dex pushed off the wall and patted him on the back. "I'll let you two lovebirds get back to having fun in your honeymoon suite," he teased them.

"Yeah, right," Lynda voiced tonelessly. "It's great being undercover with Ishikawa, but I'm already spoken for, thank you."

"Me too," Ishikawa said, which was news to Dex. Last he knew, the man had sworn off relationships following two failed marriages. Had he been holding out on them? "My horse, Isabella, is the love of my life these days," he explained. "Between her and this job, there's not much room for romance outside of pretend."

"Got it." Dex tried to resist grinning, but failed miserably. He turned his thoughts to the mission at hand. "I'll show myself out."

Half an hour later, Dex met up with Katrina's assistant manager, with whom she shared an office.

"You're a man of many talents," Alyson said from her desk. "Katrina told me she'd asked you to look into the mysterious note."

Dex acknowledged this. "I understand that you were out of the office for approximately fifteen minutes when the note was discovered?"

"Yes, that's right."

"And where were you during that time frame?" he questioned, sitting on a corner of the desk.

"At the front desk," she answered surely. "Like Katrina, working at the lodge requires wearing multiple hats at once."

He didn't doubt that, and tried to imagine what it took to run a successful business in a resort setting. Would outside lures tempt one looking for added sources of revenue? "Other than you and Katrina, who else would have valid reasons to go into the office?"

Alyson sat back thoughtfully. "Someone from housekeeping, maintenance or landscaping," she suggested. "As well as other staff who may have needed to talk to Katrina or me about a problem. Could have been anyone, really. We've always made ourselves accessible in the Hawaiian spirit of family."

Was this a familial thing? Dex wondered. Or something far more nefarious? "Did Joseph Sizemore ever receive any threats that you're aware of?"

Her curly lashes fluttered. "Not that I can think of. He never seemed to me to be under any strain, other than the usual in running a business."

Dex leaned forward. "Do you buy the notion that his death was no accident?"

"It's not for me to say," she spoke pithily. "I can only go by what the authorities are saying. If someone else believes differently, I hope you can find out why."

"So do I," he said, deciding now was not the time as an undercover PI to delve into any possible connections between his death and the trafficking of drugs at the establishment.

Dex left the office and walked around the lodge a couple of times, accompanied by Barnabas, while observing other staff surreptitiously, some of whom he intended to question. It wasn't a stretch to believe that whoever left the note worked there and, as such, could have slipped in and out of Katrina's office without being noticed. On the other hand, there was an open concept to the layout, where a guest or outsider would likely not have much difficulty whizzing in and out of the office with no one being the wiser, in the absence of surveillance cameras. Dex considered that someone knowledgeable about

Joseph Sizemore's circumstances had real information to push back against the official read on his
death. So, was this person a friend or foe who meant
Katrina harm if she didn't go along with the pro-
gram, whatever that might be?

"I DON'T TRUST the piano player!" Gordon set his jaw
as he got Katrina's attention when she stepped inside
the Kahiko Lounge.

"Why not?" She favored the bartender with a curious look.

"I caught him snooping around with that dog of
his."

Katrina smiled thinly. "He wasn't snooping
around. Dex is working for me," she said evasively.

"He wasn't on the piano," Gordon said curtly.

"I know." She debated whether or not to let him
in on Dex's new mission. As Joseph's friend, surely
he would understand her need to know exactly how
her husband died? Katrina peered at the bartender.
Was he the one who left the mysterious message? "I
hired Dex as a private investigator," she confessed,
"his main profession."

Gordon's thick brows knitted. "Why would you
do that?"

"Someone left a note in my office claiming that
Joseph's death was no accident—but murder."

"What?" His jaw dropped. "And you believe
that?"

"I don't know." Her voice weakened. "I need to

find out who left the note." She paused, gazing at him. "It wasn't you, was it?"

"No." Gordon shook his head swiftly. "If I felt that someone had killed Joseph, I would have had the courage to tell you to your face."

"Thought so." Katrina nodded. "But someone did leave it and may know something the authorities missed."

"Why would someone want to harm Joseph?" he questioned, scratching the hair on his chin.

It was a question she'd asked herself more than once. As far as she knew, her husband was not on someone's radar to kill. But then, she might have thought the same thing about Roxanne before the police said that someone had murdered her. Maybe the same person or persons had gone after Joseph as well. Which made Katrina wonder if it was possible that he was into something she wasn't privy to. Could he have kept a secret from her so powerful that it got him killed?

"I have no idea," she told Gordon. "Maybe the note was a hoax. As Joseph's friend, I'll keep you informed if Dex learns anything."

"Mahalo." He sighed thoughtfully. "Still not sure I trust Dex. There's something about the man that just doesn't seem quite right."

"I'm sure it's just your imagination." Katrina smiled at him, even as she wondered if her new employee was everything he appeared to be. He had given her no reason to believe otherwise, in spite of Gordon's uncomfortableness with him. That included the fact that Dex's employment with the private detective agency checked out. And there was no denying his skills on the piano. Or, for that matter, his ability to charm her through his good looks, smooth style and even physical touch, if she were honest about it, remembering how she'd tingled when he'd removed the loose hair from her face earlier. Katrina felt her face turning red, while keeping this to herself. "I'll let you get back to it. Catch you later."

After checking in with housekeeping and the landscaping workers, Katrina headed outside to run a few errands. In her private parking space, she hopped into a white Nissan Sentra, started it and drove off. Still occupying her thoughts was the eerie note someone left her. Would Dex be able to track down the sender? Or was this task above his pay grade? Especially if it was a onetime thing and destined to be forever a mystery. As she pondered this, Katrina moved onto Maluhia Road, en route to Lihue, the island's commercial hub and home to Nawiliwili Harbor. No sooner had she begun the drive and turned her thoughts elsewhere, when she spotted a vehicle in her rearview mirror that seemed to be too close for comfort. Peering, she couldn't make out the driver, but saw that the car was black. A Jeep Grand Cherokee, she believed.

"What's your problem?" she spoke out loud, as if the driver could hear her. Katrina sped up, more than she was comfortable with. She recalled that another car was said to have been involved in Roxanne's fatal crash. Was this the same vehicle? Did the driver intend to rear-end her and force her into crashing? Her heart skipped a beat as Katrina fully expected the vehicle to come right up to her again and try to kill her. But then she risked a dangerous maneuver in swiveling her neck around to get a better look at her potential assailant and was surprised to see that the person had dropped back, making it clear that he or she was no longer a threat. Had that been the case all along? Had her imagination run away with itself?

Since when had she become so paranoid? Probably when her husband and housekeeper died less than six months apart. It didn't help matters any when someone left the chilling note claiming that Joseph had been murdered and intimating that she might be next. How was she supposed to respond to that? Maybe by waiting to see if Dex came up with anything before jumping to conclusions. Katrina pressed down on the brake, slowing her momentum to the speed limit. She glanced up at the rearview mirror again. The other car had apparently vanished, as though it had never been on her bumper in the first place.

After stopping off at a shopping center on Rice Street, Katrina casually walked through the mall with her bags. Without warning, once again she had a feeling of being watched. Looking over her shoulder, she spotted a dark-haired, white-skinned, tall, well-built man, maybe in his early forties, wearing a moss-colored Henley T-shirt, jeans and high-top black sneakers. He seemed to be keeping pace, but made no effort to close the distance between them. And yet she sensed that he was still following her. Wearing sling-back heel clogs, she picked up the pace and headed for the exit, at which point she planned a mad dash for her car, while hoping he didn't get to her first.

As she glanced back once more, heart pounding, Katrina saw that the man was still in pursuit. Or appeared to be. She considered ducking into a shop and asking the clerk to call the police, but quickly realized that there was no law against walking in a mall. So she decided to take her chances outside, praying he wasn't armed and prepared to use the weapon against her. Walking as fast as she was, Katrina managed to get her feet tangled and lost her balance. She felt herself start to fall, realizing it was all the man needed to catch up to her.

But instead of going down, perhaps flat on her face, Katrina found herself in the sturdy arms of none other than Dex, who seemed just as surprised and unsettled as she was.

IF THIS WERE any other time or situation, Dex might have found Katrina the perfect fit in his arms and would never want to let her go. But it was the here and now and, from the looks of things, she was in a hurry to vacate the mall just as he was entering it.

"Going somewhere?" he joked, though suspecting she was anything but in a playful mood.

Managing to regain her footing while holding on to her bags, her long hair straddling her shoulders loosely, Katrina stammered, "A man was following me."

"What man?"

"That one…" she uttered, darting her eyes as if expecting someone to approach them at any second.

Dex gazed in the direction from which she had come and saw only an elderly woman walking slowly but surely. "There is no man," he told her.

Katrina colored. "He was there," she insisted. "He must have gone into one of the stores when he saw you."

"Hmm…" Dex studied the various shops nearby and considered looking in each and every one, but suspected that it would likely be a wasted effort. "Well, he's gone now."

She frowned at him. "You don't believe me, do you?"

"I believe you believe it," he responded flatly. "That counts in my book, especially coming after the enigmatic note you found." Dex gazed again over her shoulder, hoping to catch someone trying to run away. "What did the man look like?"

"He was a white male, tall and fit, with dark hair," she described him in generic terms, "late thirties or early forties, I'm guessing." She made a face. "Sorry, but I wasn't exactly in a position to get a read on his physical characteristics."

"Don't apologize," Dex said understandingly. "Did he say anything to you?"

"No," Katrina admitted, as though he should have. "He just followed me practically the length of the mall, but seemed in no hurry to bridge the gap between us. I didn't give him time to change that reckoning. Especially after I thought a black Jeep Grand Cherokee had been following me on the way to the mall, before seeming to fall back in with other traffic…" She sighed. "That's when I ran into you…"

"Good thing I showed up when I did." Dex hoped that didn't come across as flippant, knowing that she perceived herself in real danger and he had no reason to dismiss this out of hand. Especially considering that Roxanne Yamamoto had been murdered in the midst of a drug-trafficking related investigation at the Maoli Lodge. With Joseph Sizemore a potential homicide victim too, why couldn't his widow also be targeted?

Katrina regarded him with suspicion. "What are you doing here anyway?"

"I thought I'd pay Larry Nakanishi a visit at his shop in the mall," Dex responded by way of explaining his presence. Her features instantly relaxed as she understood he wasn't following her too. "After making little headway with the staff members I've spoken with, I was hoping that, as the last person to see your husband alive, Nakanishi might know something about the note. Since you're here, care to tag along?" Dex also felt that was a good idea, so he could keep an eye on her in case the man who was following her should resurface while she was away from the lodge.

"Yes, I'd like that," she spoke eagerly, and he suspected it was as much about feeling safe in his company as needing some answers from the one person who may be in a position to provide them.

"Let me help you with those bags," he said, grabbing two of the three before she could turn him down.

"Thanks." She forced a smile, then said pensively, "Larry's store is down this way."

KATRINA WAS ADMITTEDLY comforted in having Dex by her side as they headed toward Larry's Aquatic Shop. Had he not arrived at just the right time, things could have gone terribly wrong. And yet, if she were being truthful about it, the whole thing regarding the stalker and car following her could have been a big nothing burger. Or, only her imagination. After all, in spite of the scary note and her sense of unrest, in reality no one had actually tried to harm her. Had they? One little message, no matter how unsettling, needn't upend her entire life. Still, she was grateful to have her private eye and pianist as a sort of devilishly handsome protector. At least for the time being. Also, if Larry was responsible for leaving the note, he owed her—and Joseph's memory—some type of explanation.

They walked into the shop where Joseph had first met and struck up a friendship with Larry Nakanishi, based on their love for going out in the water. It was Larry's suggestion, Katrina recalled, that they go kayaking that fateful day. Could he have been responsible for Joseph's death? She studied the man as he stood behind the counter seemingly deep in thoughts of his own. In his midthirties, Larry was slender and of medium height. He had a dark brown mohawk haircut and a fisherman's anchor black goatee.

"That him?" Dex asked her.

"Yes, that's Larry," Katrina confirmed, as he turned their way.

"Katrina..." His voice wavered. "Aloha."

"Hi, Larry." She kept her own tone measured. "This is Dex. He's a private investigator," she added, hoping to leverage it in pressuring him to speak up if the store owner was holding back on anything.

"Hey," Larry muttered, eyeing him warily. "What's up?"

"Do you have a sec?" she asked in a friendly tone.

"Sure." He folded his arms guardedly. "Everything okay?"

"Not really. Someone left me a message saying that Joseph's death was not an accident."

Larry unfolded his arms. "Not sure I understand..."

"The note said that he was murdered," Dex said

bluntly. "And also warned Katrina to watch her back." He peered at Larry. "You wouldn't know anything about this, would you?"

"Why would I?" Larry's lips pursed. "It's bogus that Joseph was murdered. I was there. The shore break wave knocked him out of the kayak and he struggled to get back in. I tried to help, but he went under and drifted out to sea. By the time his body was found, it was too late." Larry eyed Katrina. "Someone's messing with you, but it's not me. Joseph was my friend. I thought you were too."

Katrina thought so too. Maybe they were barking up the wrong tree in suspecting him of leaving the note. "Sorry," she apologized. "Since you were with Joseph before he died, I was hoping you might know something about this."

"Wish I did," he said. "I have no idea why someone would leave you such a note."

Dex moved closer to the counter. "Do you know if anyone had a beef with Sizemore?"

Larry hedged. "Not enough to want to kill him," he argued.

"What about maybe to send a message that may have gone too far?"

He shrugged. "The Joseph I knew could rub some people the wrong way because of his competitive nature. But he never came to blows with anyone in my presence. I can't imagine someone wanting him dead."

Katrina was of the same mind here. Yet someone wanted her to believe that was the case. If not Larry, then who? "Someone has been following me," she told him. At least she believed this was true. "In this very mall, a man pursued me… You might know him," she said, admittedly grasping at straws, and described the man.

Larry scratched his goatee musingly. "Doesn't ring a bell. But the description is pretty vague. Sorry I can't be of more help."

"Me too." She frowned and again wondered if the entire note thing was someone's idea of entertainment to watch her squirm.

"Well, I have a customer over there I need to take care of," he said.

Katrina followed his gaze, thinking that it might be the person who had followed her in the mall. Instead, it was a much older Hawaiian man. She wrinkled her nose and faced Larry. "If anything comes to mind…"

"I'll let you know," he promised.

When they'd stepped outside, Dex asked Katrina pointedly, "Do you think Nakanishi was on the level?"

"Yes, I think so," she told him. "I don't see what he would gain by alleging that Joseph was murdered and then denying he left the note. Especially when he wasn't the man who was following me…and possibly the same person who wrote the message."

"Good point, but Nakanishi did look a bit uncomfortable, as if hiding something," he hinted. "Could be that I'm simply misreading him in looking for something that isn't there."

"Hmm… So, what now?"

Dex was still holding two of her bags as he said succinctly, "Guess that puts us back to square one."

"Meaning…?" She looked up at him, hopeful that a dead end wasn't the same as giving up what he may have seen as nothing more than a wild-goose chase.

"Meaning I won't stop until you have some answers, good or bad."

Katrina breathed a sigh of relief that at least he wasn't ready to write her off. They reached her car and she popped the trunk so they could put the bags in. She thanked Dex again for coming to her rescue. "With any luck, I'll make it back to the lodge without someone trailing me—"

"Actually, there will be someone trailing you," he said firmly. "Me. Luck aside, I'll make sure you get back safe and sound and then be on my way."

She nodded, finding herself wishing he was around all the time for her safety and his sheer physical presence that was starting to work on her, whether he knew it or not. Was this a good thing? Or was she only setting herself up for a big fall as a lonely but still alive widow who might not be ready for a serious romance. Particularly with a man who hadn't given her any real indication that he was interested in anything more than working for her. Maybe it was better that way, as she tried to juggle her busy life as a lodge owner with the mysteries that had suddenly emerged about her late husband's untimely passing.

Chapter Five

After seeing to it that Katrina got back to the lodge without someone stalking her, Dex walked her to her suite and helped bring the bags inside. While he probably should have checked himself at the door, he couldn't resist the opportunity to catch a glimpse of the personal space she occupied at the lodge. "Nice," he said, and imagined her living there alone and possibly lonely, as he set the bags down.

"Mahalo. Took a while to completely furnish, but I like it." Katrina looked comfortable in her element, though Dex could still tell that she was troubled by the recent events that had her on edge. As was he, unable to shake the feeling that what she was going through was somehow connected to his undercover investigation, which increased the stakes even more. "Can I get you something to drink?"

They were standing close enough that Dex could actually kiss Katrina if he had a mind to. While the man in him, clearly attracted to her in ways he struggled to control, wanted nothing more than to throw the playbook out the window when it came to suspects, his more sensible side told him to resist making a move that could undermine the investigation into Roxanne's death. Not to mention the possibility that the Maoli Lodge was a front for drug trafficking on the island. "I need to get back to my place and feed Barnabas," Dex said, declining the invite, as he took a step away from her. He may have read disappointment in her face, prompting him to ask, out of curiosity, "So, how were things between you and your husband?"

Her lips twitched thoughtfully. "If you're asking did I love Joseph when he died?—the answer is yes, I did love him." She paused. "Not sure, though, that I was still in love with him. Does that make sense?"

"Yeah, it does," he told her sincerely.

"Does that make me a bad wife or widow?"

"Not at all." Dex met her eyes. "Some relationships can start to lose steam over time."

She held his gaze. "I suppose."

"Part of life." He gave her a tender smile. "Can I take a rain check on that drink?"

"Of course." Her eyes lit up. "Anytime."

Dex nodded at the thought and found himself wondering what it would be like to get her into bed. Something told him he wouldn't be any more disappointed than she would be, were the opportunity to ever present itself. Dropping his temperature down a notch, Dex said in a professional manner, "If you happen to see the man who was following you again, let me know."

She nodded uneasily. "I will."

"Probably not a bad idea to avoid traveling away from the lodge by yourself for the time being," he strongly suggested, "till we can get a better handle on the note and the person who may be tracking you."

"I hear you and agree," she told him, running a hand through her hair. "I promise not to go venturing out alone until the coast is clear."

Dex grinned with satisfaction. "I'll see you tomorrow, boss," he said lightheartedly, and left.

BARNABAS ZIGZAGGED IN the backyard, as though on an obstacle course around avocado, lemon, lychee and papaya trees, which the K-9 operative dog handled masterfully in the absence of his real duties, as he went after the ball Dex threw for exercise. "Good boy," he applauded his canine and loyal friend, as Barnabas mouthed the ball and brought it back to him; whereby Dex threw it again for him to fetch. Once they had gotten this out of their systems, they headed back inside the cottage. There, Barnabas was fed, while Dex had a couple of slices of pepperoni, sausage and pineapple pizza and a beer. He updated Lynda and Ishikawa on his progress, or lack thereof, in locating the note writer. He also gave them a description of the man who Katrina said was following her, along with the dark Jeep Grand Cherokee she believed was tracking her, presumably driven by the same man. Finding out both their identities, if not the same person, was key to perhaps linking Joseph Sizemore's death to that of Agent Yamamoto in relation to trafficking of drugs at the lodge.

Dex gave the case a rest as he hopped into the shower. He wondered about Katrina and how good they could be together. Whether or not they ever got to put that to the test remained to be seen. He preferred not to look too far ahead, with things as they were in both their lives. Still, a man could dream a little. Couldn't he?

In the morning, after a mostly sleepless night, Dex went for a brisk walk with Barnabas before meeting Agents Krause and Ishikawa at the Kauai Police Department on Kaana Street in Lihue for the Drug Task Force briefing. It was held in a conference room and Dex ran into some familiar faces between other DEA agents, FBI, IRS and US Postal inspectors represented; he met members of the PD's vice section for the second time since arriving on Kauai. The fact that everyone seemed on the same page meant a lot to him, as Dex understood that complex multiagency, multistate operations such as this one involving the trafficking of illicit drugs required cooperation, along with patience.

Admittedly, he was short on the latter, as bringing to justice those responsible for the death of Roxanne Yamamoto was front and center with Dex. Along with whether or not Joseph Sizemore's death truly was a homicide, and if someone was after Katrina as well. The idea of the lovely lodge owner falling prey to a killer was something Dex had started to take personally. He would be damned if he let that happen. Even if her own innocence in drug trafficking had yet to be established, in getting to know her so far, he sensed she had no involvement in the criminal activity. Could the same be said of Sizemore before his demise? If so, was the connection there?

As if reading Dex's mind, Ishikawa whispered from the seat beside him, "By the way, we came up with nothing in the way of fingerprints from the note. Pulling DNA from it will take a little longer, but I wouldn't hold my breath on anything coming from it either."

"What a shock," Dex said wryly. "Maybe whoever left the note will do us a favor the next time around and give us something to help identify them. Obviously, I'm really hoping it's the last Katrina will hear from the person," he made clear.

"Don't count on it." Lynda threw cold water on that, sitting on the other side of Dex. "If this unsub truly believes what he or she says and is not tossing garbage at the lady just to push her buttons, then Katrina is likely to hear from them again."

That's what I'm afraid of, Dex told himself, as he considered the impact of such on the investigation. He homed in on Kauai PD Vice's veteran detective Clayton Pietz, who was the lead local investigator of the case with a proven record of drug-trafficking interdiction. Thirtysomething, tall and slender, he had a dark buzz-cut fade hairstyle and horseshoe mustache.

Pietz stood by a large touch screen monitor and updated them on the investigation. "I don't think I need to tell any of you here that West Coast and international drug-trafficking gangs and organizations, attracted to the year-round great weather and drug use among tourists, are flocking to Hawaii, pedaling everything, including lethal fentanyl-laced meth, heroin and opioids." He switched from a picturesque image to that of various drugs with a Hawaiian backdrop. "Here on Kauai, we're being hit just as hard as the other islands, with illicit drugs being smuggled in and out at a premium, moved around in an effort to avoid detection and apprehension of the traffickers, and often controlled by well-armed thugs. Our job is to break up these highly profitable operations whenever possible and, when not, put a serious dent in them so they think twice about doing business on Kauai."

Pietz touched the screen and showed various locations on the island, while he said, "We believe that traffickers have chosen different sites to hold, display and distribute illegal drugs, including the Maoli Lodge, which the owners may or may not have been aware of." He put a photograph of Roxanne on the screen. "As you know, a member of our Task Force, DEA Agent Roxanne Yamamoto, was killed last month during an undercover assignment in apparent retaliation by traffickers for doing her job in trying to build a case against them. We're doing everything we can to bring her killer or killers to justice. Assisting in this regard is DEA special agent Dex Adair and agents Lynda Krause and Sylvester Ishikawa. On behalf of Agent Yamamoto, you've got our full support."

That was just what Dex needed to hear, as he was determined to get to the bottom of Roxanne's death and how it fit with the other dynamics of the investigation. He watched as US Postal Inspector Pauline Taomoto took Pietz's place. Fortysomething and slim, with an ash-blond shag, she connected the dots between the drug bust in Downtown Los Angeles and trafficking on Kauai.

"As part of this wide-ranging drug operation, some of the same players have been involved in the attempted shipping of packages of crystal meth from LA to the island," Pauline was saying, "which we were able to intercept with the assistance of a no-nonsense drug detection K-9 named Kimiko. To make a long story shorter, with the illicit goods in our possession, along with damaging calls and text messages between suspects, we're building a case against them that will likely result in lengthy prison sentences."

This was music to everyone's ears, including Dex's. After the briefing wrapped up, he sent Lynda and Ishikawa to get more from Pauline on the case being made against the traffickers in Southern California and Kauai and linking it to their own investigation. Dex met with Detective Pietz in his spacious office with a picture window for some follow-up questions.

"Have a seat," he said casually, blue-gray eyes upon Dex while sitting in a brown high-backed chair at an oak desk.

Dex sat across from him on a beige task chair, noting a framed photograph on the wall of Pietz with his wife and a young son. Another framed pic held a commendation he received for his work with drug-related investigations and organized crime. Without any small talk, Dex went right at it in seeking any new leads in the probe into Roxanne's death. "Where are we in the investigation?"

"We're following some paths that should soon result in one or more arrests," Pietz said, leaning back with his large hands pressed together.

"Can you be more specific?" Dex asked, narrowing his gaze.

"Yeah, specifically, we're homing in on an ex-con who we think may've cut the brake lines of the car Agent Yamamoto was driving that night. I can't tell you much more right now, other than that we're attempting to establish who he may have been working for and how far up the chain this goes…"

"Where does the Maoli Lodge fit into this?"

Pietz ran a hand across his mustache. "As of now, we believe it may be a drop-off point for drugs and drug money that is quickly moved to other more secure locations for handling and distribution. It's still being investigated."

"And also got Agent Yamamoto killed," Dex pointed out hotly, not wanting her death to be undermined in any way.

"I understand that and we're not cutting any corners to nail the unsub," Pietz insisted calmly. "We're all on the same page here, Adair."

"Good to know." Dex realized he may have overreacted. He had no beef with the detective and wanted to work with him for the common good. "Have you been able to tie Joseph Sizemore to drug trafficking?"

Pietz jutted his chin. "Not in so many words."

"What does that mean?" Dex pressed.

"It means that, as of now, we have no solid evidence that Sizemore was trafficking in drugs before his kayaking accident. But we are aware that he was having money problems in running the lodge. Whether he financed it with dirty money has yet to be determined."

Money troubles? Dex wondered if Katrina was aware of this. And if the lodge could still be under water and under pressure from drug traffickers or other criminals. "What about Sizemore's widow?"

"We haven't been able to make a case for her being involved in any illicit activities or Agent Yamamoto's death," Pietz told him frankly, which allowed Dex to breathe a sigh of relief. Clearing Katrina of any wrongdoing would make it easier to be around her without having to wonder if there was something sinister below the attractive surface to her.

"Someone's been following Katrina Sizemore," he told the detective thoughtfully.

Pietz lifted a brow. "What, you mean like stalking her?"

"Yeah, you could say that." Dex took a breath. "This comes after she was left a note saying that Sizemore's death wasn't an accident, but murder, with the implication that Katrina could be next."

"That's news to me," Pietz contended.

"You mean that Sizemore's death may not have been accidental or the note?" Dex pressed his shoes against the brown carpet tile.

"Both. The autopsy report indicated that the man drowned as a result of his kayak capsizing. I have no reason to believe otherwise." Pietz glanced out the window and back. "As for the stalker and note, neither came from this office, I can promise you. If someone is after Katrina Sizemore, it's not related to our investigation."

Dex wasn't sure he bought that, given the correlation between one thing and another. But in the absence of anything to push back, he thought it best to leave it alone right now. At least insofar as pressing for answers the detective apparently didn't have. Instead, Dex would channel his focus toward Katrina and her safety, having been given a whole new reason to cozy up to her now that she was off the radar as a suspect in Roxanne's murder.

"Aloha and welcome to the Maoli Lodge," Katrina greeted her newest guests. They were an attractive family of four, having ventured to the island all the way from Dublin, Ireland, for vacation. Someday, she hoped to return the favor, welcoming the opportunity to visit Ireland and elsewhere in Europe as well as Australia and New Zealand. She and Joseph had talked about it as something to do down the line once they were established on Kauai. But then the dreams had been shattered and any such plans for herself were put on hold.

After checking the Byrnes family in, Katrina used a pause in the action to check her cell phone. For whatever reason, she had hoped to hear from Dex. Why? Maybe because they had come so close to kissing yesterday after he'd walked her back to her suite. And what if he had? How might that have changed the dynamic of their, up to this point, strictly working relationship? She wasn't sure, but wouldn't run away from the fact that the pianist and private investigator did stir something in her and maybe it wouldn't be such a bad thing to see where it could lead.

Her mind pivoted to the man who she believed was following her the day before. Who was he? Had he stayed at the lodge and somehow become fixated on her? Or did it have something—or everything—to do with the note she received? When another guest showed up to check in, Katrina dropped that train of thought and put on her hospitable smile as she laid eyes on the tall and thin Hawaiian girl who looked to be in her teens with long, straight raven hair. "Are you Katrina Sizemore?" she asked nervously.

"Yes, that's me," Katrina said, looking at her curiously.

"I was told to give this to you…" She handed her a folded piece of paper.

A chill ran through Katrina. "Who told you?"

The teenager tensed. "Just a man. He gave me ten bucks to give that to you…told me not to open it."

"What did he look like?" Katrina demanded, narrowing her eyes.

"I don't know," she shrugged. "Tall, muscular, I guess. Had dark hair and was wearing shades."

That had to be the same man who was following me, Katrina thought with dread. Had he been inside the lodge, watching her as she had sensed someone doing? Where was he now? She glared at the teen. "Can you show him to me?"

"Nope, sorry. He got in a Jeep afterward and drove off."

Had to be the same Jeep Grand Cherokee that trailed me to the mall, Katrina told herself undoubtedly. "Was he with anyone in the Jeep?"

"Don't know. Couldn't see inside." The girl looked jittery. "I have to go."

Katrina nodded understandingly, realizing that she was merely a messenger who this mysterious man used to further conceal his identity. She watched as the teen walked outside and then started to run, as though she couldn't get away fast enough. Only then did Katrina look down at the still folded note in her hands, almost afraid to open it. But she was more afraid not to see what he had to say next about Joseph and her. Unfolding the note with shaky fingers, she read.

Joseph Sizemore died as the result of an intentional drug overdose, whether you choose to believe it or not. Drowning only masked the truth about his murder. Speaking of truth, trust no one. That includes your pianist and so-called protector. He's not who you think he is.

Katrina dropped the note on the counter, as if it were a hot coal, while trying to come to grips with its portentous message. Drug overdose homicide? Trust no one? Could Dex actually be involved in the murder of Joseph, while pretending to be someone she could count on for support?

"Hey," she was given a start when hearing the familiar deep voice. Katrina raised her head and stared into the handsome face of Dex Matheson, whom she was seeing in a whole new and disturbing light. He was standing there beside his dog, Barnabas. "Is everything all right?" Dex asked, his tone seemingly picking up on her combination of vexation and worry.

"Just who the hell are you?" Katrina demanded, her own inflection making it clear that nothing less than the truth would suffice. And even that, she sensed, would alter the essence of whatever existed between them.

Chapter Six

Dex was admittedly speechless for a long moment as he took in the exacting question, feeling as though he had been caught red-handed. Or worse, that she could suddenly see through his facade. It was obvious to him that something—or someone—had exposed him, to one degree or another. Who? He noted the piece of paper on the counter that separated them, seemingly into a deep divide. No doubt, it was another cryptic message. Dex decided for the time being to play the innocent and pretend he was befuddled by the question. "Not sure I follow you," he said coolly, while holding on to Barnabas's leash. "I'm the same guy you hired—twice—to work for you…"

"And who are you beyond that, Dex?" Katrina peered at him through narrowed eyes. "Is that even your real name?" Before he could respond, she pushed the note toward him. "You might want to read that first."

Eager to do just that, Dex grabbed the note and read the distressing words. They threw him for a loop on more than one front. Asserting that Sizemore had been murdered, as if an authority on this rather than pure speculation, told him that someone was determined to spin a narrative contrary to the official cause of death. Equally troubling to Dex was that this same mystery writer had fingered him as an imposter, for all intents and purposes. Who could know this, apart from someone in law enforcement? Was a cop or even another DEA agent behind the notes? If so, to what end?

Dex met Katrina's hard gaze. "Where did you get this?" He held the note on a corner, in case evidence could be removed from it.

"A teenage girl gave it to me," she responded coldly. "The girl said a man, who matched the description of the one who was following me yesterday, handed it to her, along with ten dollars, and asked her to deliver it to me by name. He then got into a vehicle that sounded a lot like the Jeep Grand Cherokee that trailed me to the mall, and drove away." Katrina's mouth tightened as she planted a hand on her hip atop the green tiered maxi skirt she wore. "So, are you going to tell me who you are and why you've come to my lodge? Or do I fire you right now and ask you and your dog to vacate the premises immediately?"

Wow, she doesn't pull any punches, Dex thought, knowing that his options were slim to none at this point. Now that this can of worms had been opened, trying to come up with something plausible might only put him in a deeper hole. He needed to keep working there to further conduct his investigation. Then there was the matter of Joseph Sizemore's death that was starting to look more and more suspicious, in spite of the beliefs to the contrary. If that wasn't enough, Dex hated the thought of being kicked off the premises by someone with whom his vested interest had only grown over this short span of time. He couldn't walk away from her. At least not before trying to convince her that he was one of the good guys and one she could trust, in spite of his necessary deception.

He took a breath and asked in earnest, "Can we go somewhere and talk? Preferably in private…"

KATRINA HAD RESERVATIONS about inviting Dex to her suite. The mysterious note left her with more questions than answers. But even if she was wary of who he might be and what he was up to, something told her instinctively that Dex would not hurt her. At least not physically. Still, she owed it to herself, and maybe him too, to hear him out. He sat on one side of the rattan wicker cream-colored sectional in the great room, while she sat on the other, as if needing to keep some distance between them for the time being. Barnabas lay on the floor obediently beside his owner.

"Well, I'm listening…" Katrina gazed at Dex, trying to imagine what he had to say and how it might affect things between them.

He waited a beat and then said forthrightly, "All

right, first of all, my name's not Dex Matheson." He reached into his pocket and pulled out his identification, which included a badge, and slid it her way. "Actually, I'm DEA special agent Dex Adair. I'm here on an undercover assignment..."

Katrina's eyes popped wide as she studied his ID and found herself momentarily speechless. She had to admit, she hadn't seen that one coming. With the Drug Enforcement Administration? A special agent? Why would he need to be at her lodge? And was the dog undercover too? "You're not a private investigator?" she asked, though the answer was obvious.

"Afraid not." His voice lowered an octave. "But the piano playing is a real pastime of mine."

Under other circumstances, she might have found that amusing. But in this instance, her thoughts were less about his skills on her baby grand, good as they were, and more on the fact that he might have only been stringing her along in supposedly helping her as a PI. "I don't quite understand," she confessed, while withholding judgment. "Care to explain the ruse?"

Dex leaned forward, stretched out his long arm and retrieved the ID. He put it away and sat back thoughtfully, rubbing his chin. "I'm investigating drug trafficking on the island."

"Drug trafficking?" She frowned. "What does that have to do with my lodge?"

"We believe that traffickers may be using your lodge to distribute, disperse or hide illicit drugs," he spoke candidly.

"That's not possible," she uttered defensively. If it were true, wouldn't she have known? Or at least suspected such activity in her midst?

"A Task Force on drug trafficking on Kauai disagrees," Dex said sharply. His face darkened. "Last month, one of our agents, Roxanne Yamamoto, was murdered. You knew her as Roxanne Kitaoka—"

"Roxanne…" Katrina cringed as the implications registered as to the fate of her former housekeeper. "Are you saying…?"

"She was undercover while in your employ," Dex said bleakly. "Before Agent Yamamoto could issue her findings, she was killed."

"So, you're here to investigate her death?" Katrina asked, as the sadness of Roxanne's death took on even greater meaning and the truth of his presence began to fall into place.

"Yes." He pinched his nose. "And to continue the investigation into drug trafficking."

As he regarded her keenly, it dawned on Katrina that if Dex believed the Maoli Lodge was a site for trafficking drugs, then as its proprietor she must be suspected of participating. "Wait…" she gasped, "you don't think I'm a drug dealer or whatever, do you?" The notion that she could be involved in criminal activity didn't sit well with her.

"No, I don't," Dex answered firmly, allowing Katrina to breathe again. At least on that score. The other inferences of the lodge being a front for drug trafficking were no less disturbing. "I admit that initially, in doing my job, I needed to check you out, as part of the broader probe underway on the island. You're no longer a target of the investigation, Katrina," he claimed.

"I suppose I should be thanking you for that," she said sardonically, but was quite relieved, in fact, if true. Being targeted for something she was totally innocent of would have distressed anyone. Especially coming from someone she had actually begun to feel something for.

"Unfortunately, the probe into your lodge is still ongoing," Dex pointed out. "Now that the cat's out of the bag as to my identity, I would like us to work together."

Katrina glared at him. "You're joking, right?"

"Can you think of a better way to put this behind you and continue operations with a clean slate?" He locked eyes with her, illustrating his seriousness and forcing her to reassess her initial resistance. "If we determine that we're way off base, the investigation will move elsewhere. No questions asked. But if there is something to this, and I believe Agent Yamamoto's death adds credence to that, we both owe it to her to see this through. So, are you game?"

Katrina's resolve weakened in support of her friend Roxanne, even if she had been working undercover. "When you put it that way, yes, I'm in."

"Cool." Dex grinned and Katrina remembered her attraction to him before the big reveal. So what did that mean for them beyond his investigation?

Were the strong vibes between them only an act on
his part in the course of an undercover assignment?
"I'd like you to keep my real identity and mission to
yourself," he stressed. "The less people who know
what's going on, the better. If there is anyone on
your staff or otherwise involved with the lodge who's
trafficking drugs or committing related crimes, we
wouldn't want to tip them off and compromise the
investigation."

"I understand," she said, knowing that cooperating while not jeopardizing the case was in her best
interest as well as the lodge's. "Your secret is safe
with me," Katrina promised, and cast her gaze upon
the dog, who hadn't moved and was obviously well
trained. "So, I suppose that Barnabas is more than
just a good companion to you?"

Dex smiled. "Yes, Barnabas is part of a DEA
K-9 unit, trained in narcotic and drug detection."
He spoke proudly of the canine.

Katrina swallowed. "And has he detected any illegal drugs on the property?" She hesitated to ask,
but needed to know.

"Not yet. But then, I haven't really had a chance
to let him loose to do his thing," Dex said honestly.
"Could be that Barnabas comes up with nothing.
But that wouldn't necessarily mean you've gotten
over the hump at this point with respect to the lodge
being a front for drug trafficking. Let's just hope
for the best."

She picked up the sincerity in his tone in not wanting her lodge to be a party to drug criminality. Was this a natural reaction on his part? Or an indication that he did care for her as a person beyond his undercover work? Did it make a difference at this point, considering she had only established a rapport with him under false pretenses? Katrina considered that it was likely there were other undercover DEA agents at or around the lodge. She wouldn't ask Dex to confirm or deny, figuring it was on a need-to-know basis and, as such, he wouldn't want to blow their covers. Even for her. She wouldn't hold that against him, knowing that this was what he did for a living, whether she was entirely comfortable with it or not.

It brought Katrina back to the last note she'd been given. Or, more specifically, the insinuations about Joseph's death. Did Dex know more than he was letting on? Was there a connection to Roxanne's death and the drug-trafficking investigation? She peered at the DEA special agent. "Do you believe Joseph was murdered for being involved in drug trafficking?" she asked point-blank, the idea that he was killed by someone nauseating to her. Worse was the thought that her husband could have been dealing in drugs. Had that been the case, wouldn't she have known? If she had been privy to this, of course she would have, done her very best to put a stop to it?

Dex ran a hand along his jawline. "Someone sure as hell seems to think so," he responded ambivalently. "As you know, the official word is that your husband died in a kayaking accident with no appar-

ent foul play involved. That being said, the timing
in relation to the ongoing drug-trafficking investigation on Kauai is more than a little suspicious. It will
need to be further investigated. Particularly, in light
of the allegations made in the note you were given."
He paused, running his hand along the top of Barnabas's head. The dog was receptive. "Was Joseph
using any drugs at the time of his death?"

Katrina stared at the thought. "Two years ago, he
hurt his back while scuba diving. Joseph was pre-
scribed fentanyl to deal with the pain. As far as I
was aware, he overcame it and was no longer taking anything."

"We'll go on that assumption till I have a chat with
the medical examiner," Dex said matter-of-factly.
"Until then, let's not jump to any conclusions based
on an anonymous note, in spite of its insinuations."

"I'm trying not to," she told him. "But between
the notes and discovering that we've been under investigation for drug trafficking, it's hard not to think
that someone may have murdered Joseph, even if it
was for all the wrong reasons." Katrina extended
her chin sadly. "Same person or persons who murdered Roxanne."

"If that proves to be the case, we'll work through
it together," he offered gently.

"Okay." She looked at him and Katrina knew
that it was a sympathetic gesture on his part. Whatever happened, she needed to believe that someone
was still looking out for her. Maybe that person was

Dex, even if not the man she first thought him to be. Something inside her hoped she could still get to know the *real* him.

Dex stood up. "Barnabas and I will get out of here and give you some time to process things."

Katrina rose as well and flashed her eyes. "I don't really have any choice, do I?"

He moved toward her and ran a hand along her cheek. "I'm sorry you had to be caught up in this."

"So am I." She closed her eyes for a moment and soaked in the tenderness of his touch, before opening them again. "But for the sake of everything I've worked so hard for, I am committed to doing everything I can to protect the lodge and my place on Kauai. That includes cooperating with your investigation."

"Fair enough." Dex removed his hand from her face. "I'll have the note analyzed for any prints or DNA the man may have left. Other than that, if you see him again or he tries to contact you, stay away from him and let me know about it."

She nodded. "I will."

"I still have a date with the piano this evening," he reminded her, in keeping up appearances. "So, I'll see you then."

"Aloha," she said dryly, walking him and Barnabas to the door.

Only after she was left alone did Katrina wonder where this would all end. Would the lodge, and Joseph by extension, be exonerated of any wrongdoing? Or were people she thought she could trust committing crimes behind her back and right under her nose? And what would become of any possibilities between her and Dex, now that she knew he was a DEA agent who would in all likelihood be heading back to wherever he was from once the case had ended? Would he put behind him any feelings that seemed to exist between them?

"My cover's been blown," Dex informed Lynda and Ishikawa at the cottage, as each stood with beer bottles in their hands and Barnabas looked on, appearing disinterested.

Lynda gazed at him in shock. "How?"

"Damn if I know." Dex was still trying to figure it out, short of pointing fingers. "Katrina received another note…" He slipped the plastic evidence bag out of his pocket and read the message out loud. "This was left for her by the man who's been following her. Whoever he is, he's on to me."

Ishikawa grabbed the note, reading it again. "Who the hell is this person?"

"That's what we need to find out." Dex took a sip of beer pensively. "He's obviously going out of his way to maintain a low profile."

"Think he's one of us?" Lynda questioned.

"Doesn't seem likely, if we're talking about the DEA. As for the locals or someone else on the Task Force, it's anyone's guess."

Ishikawa narrowed his eyes. "But why would any

of them want to push the homicide narrative for Sizemore's death in direct contrast to the official findings?"

"Maybe because the person disagrees with the assertion that Sizemore's death was accidental, but is not in a position to say so," Dex suggested, and thought about how this had adversely weighed on Katrina. He wanted to do whatever he could to get to the truth for her as well as himself regarding any association between the deaths of Sizemore and Roxanne.

"On the other hand," Lynda put out, tilting her beer bottle, "it could be that the note came from the person responsible for Sizemore's death and they don't want to see the truth swept under the rug."

"You mean he wants to take credit for murdering him," Ishikawa contended, "and is also sending a signal to whoever else may be involved in the drug-trafficking scheme that he means business?"

"Exactly," she said flatly.

"Any of those theories is plausible," Dex told them. "Maybe this time we'll get lucky and get some evidence off the note."

"How are things with the widow after the latest note?" Ishikawa asked.

"Not very good, I'm afraid." Dex took another gulp of his beer. "She's pretty shaken up about it, quite naturally."

"And what's the status of your undercover identity?" Lynda eyed him sidelong.

"She knows I'm a DEA special agent," he responded without batting an eye. "Once the thought that I wasn't being straight with her had been planted, I had no choice but to come clean. Or be fired. Since it was already pretty clear that Katrina was not involved in any wrongdoing, I figured she could be an asset if I revealed my real identity and mission."

"I think you're right about that," Ishikawa said, and swallowed beer. "Having someone on the inside who can be trusted is a good thing at this point."

"Does she know about us too?" Lynda faced Dex intently.

"No," he emphasized. "That's the good news. The mystery man doesn't appear to be privy to your undercover assignments. I saw no reason to divulge this to Katrina," Dex said, holding the line on a need-to-know basis. "As such, you'll be able to carry on with what you're doing while keeping an eye out for anyone suspicious lurking around."

"That works for me." Ishikawa leaned over to rub one of Barnabas's ears.

"Same here," Lynda agreed and finished off the beer.

"I'll bring Rachel up to date on where thing's stand," Dex told them, knowing the SAC would have his back in continuing the investigation, even with his cover exposed. In this instance, he welcomed being able to be up-front with Katrina, wanting her to get to know him for who he truly was and hoping to take the opportunity to get to know her better as well beyond their professional lives and tenuous circumstances.

Chapter Seven

After a mostly restless sleep, Katrina welcomed the morning sunshine and an opportunity to stretch her legs with a walk along the south shore of Poipu Beach. Considered as one of the top beaches in the country, its string of sandy crescents, cool trade winds and spectacular ocean view made the beach a favorite place for her to spend time outside the Maoli Lodge. Mindful of Dex's warning not to leave the lodge on her own as long as someone was stalking her, she was accompanied by Alyson, who routinely took advantage of the setting with daily walks to stay in shape.

I refuse to be a prisoner in my own home, Katrina thought defiantly, as her bare feet stepped across the soft sand. While heeding Dex's advice, she felt a need to be out and about relishing the setting Kauai afforded her. Honestly, she hoped the DEA special agent and his cronies were able to prove that the lodge was not a place for drug trafficking. Neither she nor Joseph, when he was alive, would have tolerated such activity. But what if traffickers were operating outside their knowledge and this had somehow cost Joseph his life? The pain at the thought was enough for Katrina to shift her focus. She gazed at the tombola splitting the two coves. Called Nukumoi Point, it was a resting place for Hawaiian monk seals, an endangered species. She admired the earless seals, while hoping they would stay protected, just as she wanted to be from anyone who may wish her harm.

"So, any more news on that weird note somebody left you?" Alyson broke into her thoughts.

Katrina, who kept in stride with her fast-walking assistant manager, smiled at her, while responding evenly, "Not yet. But Dex is still looking into it." She had refrained from mentioning the second alarming and revealing note she'd received yesterday, if only to protect Dex's cover as promised. Though she trusted Alyson, Katrina would hate for the talkative assistant manager to accidentally say something to someone that might impede the investigation. Or endanger Dex. "I don't intend to let it occupy my every waking moment," she lied.

"Good for you," Alyson told her while keeping up the brisk pace. "Joseph was a good man. If someone had truly wanted to harm him, I'm sure the authorities would be on top of it. Just as they were in deciding that Roxanne's death was the result of foul play, even if there's no reason to believe it had anything to do with her employment at the Maoli Lodge."

I'm afraid it may have had everything to do with

that, Katrina mused bleakly in thinking about Roxanne being an undercover DEA agent, like Dex, at the lodge. Had she discovered something nefarious that made her a target? Or could her death have been a random act of violence? "Let's hope not," she muttered. "We'll just have to wait and see when the investigation is completed."

"True." Alyson frowned. "Let's not freak out about it till then. Agreed?"

Katrina grinned. "Agreed." She took a breath and was able to stay in lockstep with her. Then, all of a sudden, a strange yet familiar feeling came over Katrina. As before, it seemed as though she was being watched. Her eyes darted around, expecting to see the stalker trailing them. Or ready to pounce like a leopard. She saw no one, but her heart continued to race nonetheless. Perspiration dripped beneath her armpits. Was it her imagination this time, making her go crazy?

Alyson noticed. "Hey, are you all right?"

"Yes, I'm fine," Katrina pretended. "It's just that… I thought…"

"Thought what?"

"Never mind." Katrina decided not to overreact. "It was nothing." Still, she was concerned enough to look around again. If the man who left the notes was out there lurking in the shadows, she didn't want to get caught blindsided. But there was no one there. She turned to Alyson, who had taken her cue and scanned the beach.

"Looking for someone?" she asked, inquisitiveness flickering in her eyes.

"Not really," Katrina claimed. "Just checking out who else is up and at it this morning." Rather than belabor the point and feel foolish in the process, she said the most practical thing to be on the safe side, "Anyway, we better get back to the lodge before they start to miss us."

Alyson smiled. "Whatever you say."

As they reversed course, Katrina once more looked over her shoulder for someone who wasn't there. She could only assume that Dex would come up with some answers, even if no longer working for her as a private investigator. At least, she mused, he truly was a gifted pianist, giving her this much to look forward to for as long as he cared to keep this undercover role going.

DEX STEPPED INTO the Kauai County Medical Examiner and Coroner's office on Kuhio Highway in Lihue, where he was greeted by the ME herself. Francesca Espanto was in her early forties and petite, with medium-length champagne blond hair in a feathered cut. She wore oval eyeglasses over brown eyes.

"Aloha," she said routinely. "I'm Dr. Espanto."

"Aloha." He was starting to catch on with some of the common Hawaiian lingo. "DEA Special Agent Adair," he said, flashing his ID for effect, after speaking with her briefly over the phone.

"You wanted to know about Joseph Sizemore's death?"

"Yes, a little more clarity on how he died." Dex mused that anything other than an accidental drowning would not only raise red flags, but be that much more difficult for Katrina to stomach. He realized, though, that the unanswered questions about foul play would be even tougher for her.

"Follow me…"

They went down a corridor and entered a nice-sized office with modern furnishings and white cement tile flooring. Francesca offered him a seat on one of two vanilla leather chairs with flip arms. She sat in an oversize red ergonomic chair at an L-shaped espresso computer desk, and pulled up the file on Sizemore on her laptop. After a moment or two, she said matter-of-factly, "Officially, Mr. Sizemore's death came as the result of drowning. As I understand it, his kayak got hit with a shore break wave, causing him to take a tumble, whereby he drowned. By all appearances, it was an accidental tragedy."

"Were there any drugs in Sizemore's system?" Dex asked, sensing there was more to the story.

"Yes." Francesca furrowed her brow as she pulled up more information. "The toxicology report revealed that Mr. Sizemore had nonlethal concentrations of fentanyl and methamphetamine in his body at the time of death."

"Hmm…" Dex recalled the mysterious note indicating with certainty that Sizemore's death was due to an OD, the drowning notwithstanding. Which was in stark contrast to Katrina's belief that he was not using any medications or drugs at the time of his death. "Could someone have deliberately administered the fentanyl or meth to Sizemore with the intention of killing him or knocking him out—had the shore break wave not beaten them to the punch—with the water finishing him off?"

Francesca stared at the question. "Without getting into the head of someone with such an intent, I suppose it's possible that someone tried to kill the victim with the fentanyl and meth," she surmised. "But had that been the case, the levels of the drugs in Joseph Sizemore's system were simply not strong enough in and of themselves to deal the decedent a fatal blow. On the other hand, it is possible that the drug combo could have been enough to render Mr. Sizemore unconscious when or after he hit the water, which then led to his drowning..."

Dex mulled that over as another thought entered his head. "Is it possible that Sizemore took the meth and fentanyl together with the intention of committing suicide? Or to help himself along while anticipating the wave, making drowning more palatable?" He recalled Detective Clayton Pietz indicating that Sizemore had run into financial difficulties. Could taking his own life been his ticket out, while ensuring that Katrina would have the money from insurance to keep the Maoli Lodge running?

"Anything's possible," the medical examiner allowed. "But again, my job is not to interpret the precise mindset of the dead, per se, rather to determine the actual cause of death and any contributory factors, while leaving a question of intent and conjecture to other professionals such as yourself, Agent Adair."

"I understand." He gave a little self-conscious grin respectfully and then stood. "Thanks for your time."

"Mahalo." She smiled back. "I'm here to help in any way I can."

Dex felt the same way. He only hoped that Katrina would accept his help in the spirit intended, even if in the process she was likely to experience more pain before things got better.

"I'VE GOT NEWS..." Dex said in a tone that told Katrina it wasn't good. Though she wanted to run away from anything that might further shake her world, she knew it wasn't a realistic option. She needed to know whatever he was willing to share, for the sake of the lodge and the memory of her late husband.

"Why don't we go out into the garden," she suggested, knowing there was a quiet place where they could talk. She led him through an assortment of flowering, spice and tropical fruit trees, and past a fish-filled pond surrounded by exotic Hawaiian plants, until reaching a wooden octagonal gazebo. They sat near each other on a cedar bench, before Katrina asked hesitantly, "What did you find out?"

Dex waited a beat and said evenly, "I spoke with the medical examiner and she's sticking with the belief that Joseph's death was due to drowning, and most likely an unfortunate accident." He waited another beat, telling Katrina that there was more to the story. "The toxicology report showed that there was fentanyl and methamphetamine in his system at the time of death, which may or may not have contributed to it…"

"Fentanyl and methamphetamine?" she uttered, as though foreign words. Had Joseph continued to use painkillers even after he had told her he had quit? Why wouldn't he have confided in her? Tried to get through his pain without overmedicating himself?

"I'm sorry," she heard the gentle words come from Dex's mouth. "I know you thought he was off the fentanyl and maybe the meth is news to you…"

Katrina reacted. "Yes, I never knew he was using meth," she admitted with frustration. "And I'd really hoped the fentanyl was behind him." She paused. "Obviously, I didn't know my husband as well as I thought I did," she muttered sadly.

"By keeping you in the dark, he was probably trying to protect you the only way he knew how," Dex suggested.

She thought about the stalker and his role in creating suspicion about how Joseph died. "What about the notes insisting there was foul play involved in Joseph's death?"

Dex angled his head and had a thoughtful look. "I'm guessing that whoever has been leaving you the notes has some knowledge of Joseph using the drugs—maybe his supplier or even another user—and may have been acting out of guilt or some misplaced sense of duty in believing the drugs had truly killed him."

"Perhaps," she allowed, still trying to make sense of Joseph using fentanyl again, along with meth, when he seemed to be doing so well. How could she have not known this wasn't the case? Something about this entire scenario still wasn't sitting well with her. Why was the man stalking her so adamant in his position? What did he hope to gain from this harassment? Katrina turned toward Dex, who also seemed to be wrestling with the conclusions from the medical examiner. "What if the man stalking me knows more than he's said so far about Joseph's death and something is still being missed in the official findings?" She couldn't help but think about the feeling she had this morning of being watched, even if there was no proof of that to make it worth mentioning to Dex. But that didn't mean her instincts weren't correct.

"That's possible," Dex said with a ragged sigh. "The one other person who may be in a position to know about the drug use and any intentions to commit murder would be Larry Nakanishi, the last one to see your husband alive. Maybe the fact that the stalker followed you to the very mall where he works could be more than just coincidence. They could be in this together…"

"You think?" Katrina quivered at the consideration that Larry could have aligned himself with someone stalking her. If so, to what end?

"There's only one way to find out." Dex's warm breath fell onto her cheek. "Do you have your phone?" When she nodded, he said, "Let's give Nakanishi a call right now—and let's do a video chat."

Katrina took the cell phone out of the pocket of her wide leg pants, pulled up Larry's name from her contact list and tapped the video camera icon. After a couple of rings, he accepted the video chat request.

"Aloha, Katrina." His voice was cagy. "What's going on?"

"You tell me," she said tersely. "Did you know that Joseph was using meth and fentanyl on the day he died?"

Larry's chin sagged. "Knew about the meth—we both just wanted a little buzz before going out on the kayaks—but not the fentanyl," he claimed. "I don't know anything about that."

"How long had Joseph being using meth?" Katrina questioned, not sure she believed his lack of knowledge about the fentanyl.

"As long as I've known him. Said he needed it to deal with some back pain and just to get high."

Katrina cringed at the thought that her husband had chosen to keep this from her, knowing she would have done everything in her power to get him off and away from drugs and their destructive nature. "Well, the drugs may have contributed to his death," she alleged.

A brow shot up and Larry scratched his neck. "If it's true, I'm sorry to hear it, but it's not my fault. Joseph did what he wanted."

She couldn't argue with that as the realities of the life they had and the secrets he kept with his drug use dawned on her. Gazing at Dex, who indicated with his fierce eyes that he wanted in on the conversation, Katrina turned back to Larry and said firmly, "The private investigator I'm working with would like to have a word with you—"

Before Larry could object, Dex took the phone and asked commandingly, "Where did Sizemore get the meth he used that day?" Katrina knew that, by extension, Dex was assuming the supplier could have also given Joseph synthetic fentanyl—possibly her stalker.

"Just a dude," Larry muttered shakily.

"That's not good enough, Nakanishi." Dex furrowed his forehead. "I need a name!" When Larry hesitated, Dex added while maintaining his cover, "I have friends with the DEA. I'd be happy to give them a call and have them show up at your door to see just what they might find inside. I suspect it might not go well for you or your aquatic shop..."

"All right, all right," he relented. "His name is Julio."

"Julio what?"

"He only goes by Julio," Larry contended.

"What does he look like?" Dex asked.

Katrina listened as the drug dealer named Julio

was described as an olive-skinned, brown-haired male in his early thirties. She exchanged glances with Dex, as they both realized this was not the same man who had been stalking her.

"Where can I find this Julio?" Dex demanded.

"You can't." Larry colored. "Heard he left the island in a hurry a few months back. Maybe to Oahu. As for me, after what happened to Joseph, I've been off meth for a while now, trying to clean up my act."

"For your sake, I hope you're leveling with me," Dex said in a threatening tone; then he pivoted to a more friendly voice. "While we have you, we're still looking for the man who's been stalking Katrina and seems to believe Joseph was murdered. Are you sure he's not someone you know?" Dex repeated his description, which Katrina believed was spot-on. Larry didn't buckle, insisting that he didn't recognize the man, which meant they were no closer to identifying him than before. It indicated that the stalking and messages might not be over. The thought gave her a chill.

After the conversation with Larry ended, Dex peered at Katrina and asked point-blank, "Do you think it's possible that Joseph may have taken his own life?"

Her head jerked as if she'd been hit. "You mean suicide?" she asked, though the answer was obvious.

"It's the one angle we haven't tackled," Dex said honestly. "That might explain taking fentanyl and meth at the same time he was going on a kayaking trip."

"No, Joseph would not have killed himself," Katrina said with certainty, putting aside the accidental or deliberate act of murder possibilities. At least she was trying to convince herself that, no matter what, taking such an extreme measure was not in the cards for him. "Though he may have been using drugs willingly, he still had too much to live for to simply throw it all away just like that."

Dex turned away and back, his eyes pinning on her face. "In the course of the drug-trafficking investigation, it's been discovered that Joseph was having some money issues. Do you know anything about that?"

Katrina didn't like the implication. But she couldn't allow it to throw her off-balance, even if this wasn't necessarily Dex's aim. Was it? "I'm not quite sure what you're getting at," she told him, while reading between the lines. "Yes, we've had our struggles making ends meet, like other small business owners. But through it all, we were able to balance the budget and keep things going just fine. When Joseph died, his insurance allowed me to use the payment to cover any outstanding debts and complete a few overdue repairs to the lodge with a bit left over for my savings." Her brows lowered. "If there's something else on your mind, just say it."

"All right." He drew a breath and held her steady gaze. "With the investigation still ongoing, it's possible that your husband could have engaged in drug trafficking to make enough money to help with the bills without you ever being the wiser." Dex let that settle in before continuing. "If that's true, he could have put himself in danger and lost control of the situation, resulting in his murder. Or he could have simply gotten in over his head in dealing with some bad people, or even just being overwhelmed with the finances or lack thereof in running the lodge, and decided to check out, sparing you to the extent possible, while seeing to it that his insurance would kick in to ease your burden. If you think I'm way off base here, feel free to say so."

Everything in Katrina wanted to totally disagree with all of Dex's theories: the assertion that her dead husband had taken his own life due to financial pressures or to provide her operating money from insurance upon his death; or to escape the physical pain he'd apparently still been enduring; or even aligning himself with drug traffickers in some ill-advised scheme of helping them keep their heads above water in operating the lodge. But the truth was she wasn't sure what to think at this point. Joseph had already shaken her confidence in discovering that he was using drugs illegally. What else did she not know? What other secrets would she discover about her husband of seven years that would further shake her foundation?

She took a breath and met Dex's eyes. "Maybe you're not off base," she conceded. "I simply don't know. In my heart and soul, I can't bring myself to believe the man I once loved would rather kill himself than face whatever demons he had together. But we were struggling somewhat in making ends meet and…it's possible that he could have resorted to drastic measures behind my back to do what he thought was necessary to stem the tide—" Her voice shook. "If that's true, I won't shirk from my responsibilities as a law-abiding citizen and loyal resident of Kauai to make things right in any way I can."

"You already have by cooperating with me," Dex said, placing a hand upon hers, causing Katrina to react favorably as she found her other hand overlapping his. She felt the connection throughout her entire body and maybe right into her soul.

"I can do more," she insisted, releasing his hand reluctantly. He continued to caress her other hand, which was torturously appealing. "If Joseph was dealing in drugs to bring in more money, the one person who may know about it is Gordon, whom he seemed to confide in."

Dex nodded, taking his hand back and standing. "Why don't we pay the bartender a little visit and see what he can tell us…"

Katrina agreed as she got up, while at the same time fearful of what Gordon might have to say about the man she once believed she would spend the rest of her life with. Instead, he was gone and she had to deal with the aftermath alone. For better or worse. Or might she be able to somehow come out of this

on the right side of the track with the help of a DEA
agent who seemed as much dedicated to her health
and well-being as his job and getting to the truth?

Chapter Eight

There was no getting around it as they headed out of the tropical gardens and its impressive offerings. Dex liked touching Katrina. She had such soft hands and he could only imagine the softness of the rest of her body. Not to mention, she clearly had a heart of gold. Any man would be lucky to have her as the love of his life. Joseph Sizemore had her in the palm of his hand and allowed her to slip away. Or had it been outside of his control? Did the man purposely end his life through drugs and drowning? Or, as contended in the notes left for Katrina, had someone murdered Sizemore? If so, was it because he no longer wanted to play ball with traffickers? Or had he gotten on someone else's bad side?

Dex was eager to get this resolved. He knew that was even more important to Katrina. She deserved some closure. Whether that put Sizemore in a positive or negative light, at least she could move on with her life knowing the truth. Then maybe she would be more open to starting over and having a new relationship to work on. Dex would love to be on the receiving end of that affection. But could it work when his career as a DEA special agent had him crisscrossing the states within his jurisdiction, leaving not nearly enough time to put his all into a romance with a beautiful woman who merited no less in a man?

When they entered the Kahiko Lounge, Gordon Guerrero was busy unboxing liquor on the other side of the bar. It was obvious to Dex that the bartender didn't particularly care for him, based on their exchanges. He didn't sense that the man was interested in pursuing Katrina romantically. But maybe as a friend to her and Sizemore, Gordon hoped to protect Katrina from getting hurt. Or was it more about wanting to make sure his cousin's wife had a place to return to after her maternity leave was up? As it was, Dex had run a criminal background check on Guerrero in relation to their drug-trafficking probe. Other than a DUI five years ago, he saw no red flags that suggested he was dealing in drugs on the side while bartending.

"Hey," Katrina said, walking up to the counter.

"Hey." Gordon stopped doing what he was doing. He regarded Dex uneasily.

"Can we talk to you for a moment?" she asked.

"Yeah." He leaned against the counter. "What do you need?"

"Information," she put out solidly.

"What kind of information?"

"Did Joseph ever mention anything to you about money problems?"

Gordon shrugged. "Yeah, I suppose, from time to time. Comes with the territory. Why do you ask?"

"Because I need to know if he was in any kind of trouble," Katrina answered bluntly.

"Trouble?" The bartender grabbed a clean glass and a cloth to dry it, which Dex interpreted as a sign of nervousness. Or was it guilt by association?

She peered at Gordon. "Do you know if Joseph was selling drugs at the lodge—or somewhere else?"

"No, not that I know of." His brows descended. "Why would you think that?"

"Because he had drugs in his system at the time of death," she replied, "according to the medical examiner. Joseph was also quite worried about our finances. If this resulted in his trafficking drugs, I need to know. So does Dex here…" Dex cringed when he thought she might blow his cover. Instead, Katrina merely said truthfully, "Someone has been stalking me. I believe it's the same person who's been leaving me notes, indicating that Joseph was the victim of foul play. As a PI, Dex has learned that the authorities are looking into drug trafficking on the island. Maybe even taking place at the Maoli Lodge. If you know anything about this and Joseph's involvement, you need to tell me, Gordon."

"If it's true, it's only a matter of time before the police piece it together—" Dex decided to up the ante

"—and bring down anyone who is an accomplice to the trafficking of drugs on Kauai soil…"

"Joseph never indicated to me that he was dealing drugs," Gordon maintained, sneering at him. "Whether he was using or not to get through the day, he wouldn't have disrespected the land or you, Katrina," he emphasized, "by going down that path." The bartender drew a sharp breath. "But Joseph did confide in me that he was short on funds and needed to buy some time till business picked up, since he wasn't able to get anything more from the bank. I suggested he try calling a local moneylender I know…"

Dex's mouth turned down. "You mean a loan shark?"

Gordon's chin jutted. "Yeah, I guess."

"Did Joseph get in touch with him?" Katrina demanded.

"I believe so."

"We need the person's name and address," Dex told the bartender, making it clear it wasn't a casual request. Gordon wasted no time in giving them what they needed.

After leaving the lounge, Dex told Katrina, "I'll go talk to the loan shark and see if Joseph borrowed money from him with a high interest rate." Though far from advisable, if true, it would at least make it less likely that Sizemore turned to trafficking drugs for profit to fund his business or drug habit.

"I'm coming with you," she said firmly.

"Not sure that's such a good idea." As a DEA agent in an official capacity, Dex was hesitant to bring a civilian into the case. Especially Sizemore's widow.

"I have to beg to differ there." Katrina gave him a hard look that indicated she meant business. "Joseph was my husband. I need to find this out for myself—with or without you." She sighed. "I'm sure you understand."

As it became clear to him that she was as stubborn as he was, perhaps more so, Dex didn't fight it. "Yes, I think I do. Just be prepared for whatever may come out of this," he warned in the nicest manner possible.

"I could say the same to you, Agent Adair." She steeled herself for any pushback. "Let's just get this over with."

Dex grinned, liking this unflappable side of her. He imagined that would come in handy under other more intimate circumstances. But for now, they were on a mission to either clear her late husband of any wrongdoing relative to the drug-trafficking probe or discover that Sizemore had dug himself an even deeper hole that could well have cost Roxanne her life.

KATRINA HAD VOLUNTEERED to drive, seeing that she knew the island better than Dex, to get to the loan shark's office more quickly. He surprised her by agreeing to ride along. Now she was on pins and needles, wondering if Joseph had leveraged the lodge itself in borrowing against it, potentially defaulting and putting her livelihood at risk. Though in her mind the books were balancing each month, what if Joseph had hidden his loans from her and had a separate set of books that had her well under water, even with the insurance payout that had seemingly given her the necessary breathing room to continue operating the lodge effectively with enough left over for savings.

I can't freak out about this, Katrina mused, willing herself to keep her thoughts in check as she drove down Maluhia Road. At least not until they spoke with the moneylender and determined whether or not Joseph had followed through in contacting him. And assessed what he might have done had his house of cards come crashing down upon him. Along with her.

"How are you holding up?" she heard Dex's deep voice ask with concern.

"I'll reserve comment on that for now, if you don't mind," Katrina told him, figuring there was no need to sugarcoat some of the emotions she was feeling at the moment in speculating whether or not the man she was married to had gone too far in making poor decisions. Better to wait and see just what she might be up against, as though the allegation of drug trafficking at the lodge wasn't bad enough.

"I don't mind at all," Dex assured her from the passenger seat. "But just so you know, however this goes, you're in the clear and I won't let the investigation impede your ability to run the Maoli Lodge and look ahead."

"Mahalo." Katrina appreciated his kind words and couldn't help but wonder what was in the cards for him in looking ahead. Did he ever plan to settle down? Or was his world of going undercover and tracking down drug offenders never to change? Was there anyone special in his life who he'd failed to mention in their mutual flirtation now that his true identity was out in the open? She glanced his way and decided to just ask boldly what was on her mind. "So, in your real world, Dex, do have a wife or girlfriend waiting back home for you to finish your latest assignment? Or is that confidential information?"

"Not confidential." He grinned at her. "There's neither a wife nor girlfriend waiting for me anywhere," he responded succinctly. "There was someone special once in my life, but it never came even close to us walking down the aisle."

"Oh…?" She wondered whether or not he got cold feet. Maybe Dex wasn't the type to commit.

"She cheated on me and seemed to think it was no big deal." He shook his head with a look of betrayal. "In any event, that was the name of that tune."

"Sorry about that," Katrina said sincerely. Though things were less than perfect between her and Joseph, she had always been faithful to him and believed the same was true from his side. Or could she be way off base here too about the man she was wed to?

"It happens," Dex muttered. "Lessons learned and all that."

"I'm sure there's someone out there for you." Did she really just say that? Katrina had always worn her heart on her sleeve. But was she telling him that she was ready, able and willing to take up with him—at least while he was around? If so, would she be able to put the past behind her as he seemed to be willing to do?

"You too," he countered surely, as though reading her thoughts, and added tellingly, "All you have to do is be willing to go the extra mile…once you're ready for that—"

Katrina allowed that to sink in, knowing her first step in that direction was to find out if Joseph had poisoned the well in destroying what was once their dream together. Only then could she truly turn the corner in regrouping. "I've gone a few extra miles for the time being," she quipped, while driving onto Kipuni Way in Kapaa, a town on the island's east side that was known for its Sleeping Giant Trail for hikers and the 151-foot Ho'olalaea Waterfall.

He chuckled. "Yeah, I can see that."

Four blocks later, Katrina pulled into the parking lot of a place called Cash to Give, wondering if she was about to encounter another disappointment in her marriage and roadblock in her business.

"You ready for this?" Dex asked in earnest.

"I have to be," she replied squarely, wanting to get it over with. Or was that even possible at this stage?

"Then let's go," he said without further ado.

They stepped inside the small, cluttered office with a dirty picture window. A sixtysomething, thickset, deeply tanned man with short thin gray hair in a brushed back style and a salt-and-pepper beard fade was seated at a computer desk that included file drawers. When he saw them, he leaned back in his black leather chair and said, "Aloha. How can I help you?"

"Are you Philip Shepherd?" Dex asked.

"Yeah, that's me. Who are you?"

"DEA Special Agent Adair," he said, flashing his ID. This surprised Katrina, but she instinctively understood that it was meant to intimidate him into cooperating. "This is Katrina Sizemore. We need to know if her late husband, Joseph Sizemore, contacted you for a loan."

Shepherd rubbed his stomach. "Afraid I'm not at liberty to give out confidential information between me and my clients, assuming he ever was one."

"I'd rethink that if I were you." Dex leaned over the desk menacingly. "I'm investigating drug trafficking on Kauai. If any loaned money turned out to be used to buy or distribute illicit drugs, that makes you an accessory. That means the feds will rain down on this place and if you have any skeletons in the closet, trust me, we'll find them…"

"Okay, okay—no need for this to go that far." Shepherd sucked in a deep breath. "The man's name doesn't actually pop out at me. Give me a moment to look him up." He started typing on his laptop. "Spell that for me?"

Katrina volunteered in doing so, adding, "He would have gotten in touch with you within the past year or so," she assumed." She hated to think that Joseph had reached such a stage of desperation to seek money from a loan shark.

"Hmm…" Shepherd muttered. "Nothing's showing up. You have a picture of your husband?"

"Yes." She took out her cell phone from a shoulder baguette bag and pulled up what was probably the last picture of Joseph. It was taken at the lodge, in the lobby, where he actually posed for her. How could she have known that he was hiding things from her even then? Katrina held the small screen up to the moneylender. "That's him," she uttered.

Shepherd needed only a moment, before saying, "Right, I remember him now… He never took out a loan."

"Why not?" Dex asked dubiously.

"Said he needed fifty grand. I told him no problem, but after I explained what I expected in return in terms of interest and date of payback in full, the man balked."

Katrina wrinkled her brow. "Are you saying Joseph never took out a loan from you?" she questioned to be sure.

"Yeah, that's what I'm saying," he reiterated and eyed her musingly. "Your husband had second thoughts, said instead he would cash in some stocks that you weren't aware he had to cover his debts. Then he left. Never saw him again."

Back in the car, Dex said, "If what Shepherd said was true, it should be easy enough to verify the sale of secret stocks to help cover debts."

Katrina was a mixture of emotions. She felt relief that her husband had apparently not followed through on taking money from a loan shark. Better still, it suggested that Joseph had not gotten himself involved in drug trafficking to make money. But the fact that he had invested in the stock market without bothering to tell her was frustrating in its own right. "How could he have not told me about the stocks?" she griped aloud.

"Maybe he wanted to wait and see how they did first before letting you in," Dex indicated, which Katrina knew was his way of trying to ease her sense of betrayal.

"Nice try, but it won't fly." She tightened her grip on the steering wheel. "If Joseph had that much of our money invested in stocks, I had every right to know about it."

"I couldn't agree more," he made clear. "That's not the way a marriage should work. On the other hand, if the return was enough to help keep the lodge running, this would seem to exonerate Joseph of trafficking drugs for capital."

"You're right." Katrina loosened her fingers on the steering wheel. "I suppose I should be thanking him for not committing crimes to prevent us from going under," she said sarcastically.

Dex faced her profile. "You should be pissed. No excuses for what he did. He screwed up. Having never run a lodge such as yours, I can't begin to know the pressures one must be under to succeed in the competitive hospitality business in a resort setting. Apparently, though, selling stocks does seem to take suicide off the table. And, as of now, the murder angle is not holding water either, as the notes maintained, the drug use notwithstanding."

"I feel relieved about that," she had to admit, in spite of her disappointment in Joseph on so many other levels. Not the least of which was his uncanny ability to pull the wool over her eyes in some of his actions and inactions. But that didn't mean she would ever want to see him be the victim of foul play. "I just want to put this behind me. Hopefully, the stalker will leave well enough alone and not continue to harass me with unfounded allegations." She considered her earlier sense of being watched. What did this person hope to gain, other than fill her with doubts about Joseph and what he may or may not have been up to, placing her in danger? Or was there some other angle to this yet to unfold?

"I hope that too," Dex said, his tone suggesting he wasn't entirely convinced that would be the case. "I'll continue to try and find out who this man is and what he wants from you. My guess is that he's merely looking for attention and singled you out as a young widow who's vulnerable for obvious reasons. So far, he seems to be stopping just short of crossing the line. Let me know if this changes or if you are otherwise contacted by him."

Katrina nodded and turned to him with a soft smile. She wondered what she would do without the handsome DEA agent and piano player. The fact that she had to ask told her how much she had grown to depend on his presence in her life, limited as it was. It scared her to think that this would likely end as soon as his investigation was completed. Yet expecting any more from him afterward would be asking too much. Wouldn't it?

Chapter Nine

"The pool maintenance tech is here," Alyson informed Katrina that afternoon as she stood at her adjustable desk. Katrina had been going over the books with a fine-tooth comb, looking for any discrepancies in the numbers that she might have missed before learning of Joseph's questionable business practices. There were no red flags, giving her some sense of solace. Later, she intended to see if there might be more stock investments made by him, other than their joint investments, that needed to be accessed. She hoped that Dex wouldn't find any illegal financial transactions along the way that could impact her livelihood. As for Joseph's drug use, the medical examiner did not believe it led to his death and this was something for Katrina to hold on to, though she would forever be left feeling disappointed that her husband had not tried harder to deal with pain management through legitimate means and allow her to help him through it.

"Katrina... Did you hear me?" Alyson said, and

repeated her information. "You wanted to know when the new guy arrived so you could make sure we were on the same page with him in terms of his work ethic and keeping the pool up and running."

"Yes, I did want to talk with him," Katrina said, snapping out of her daydreaming. "Thanks."

"Is everything okay?" the assistant manager asked. "You've seemed a bit off ever since we were on the beach this morning."

"I'm fine, Alyson." Katrina needed to keep up appearances, not wanting to bring her problems to her employees. Even one she considered a friend. At least where it concerned matters that were more of a personal nature and, thus, best kept to herself. Along with Dex, though still trying to decide if his involvement was more on the side of law enforcement or as someone who had taken it upon himself to be just as invested in her welfare. "It's been one of those days," she stated, leaving it at that.

"Tell me about it." Alyson gave her a knowing look. "Honestly, sometimes I can't tell whether I'm coming or going."

"Welcome to the club." Katrina managed a chuckle. "What's the pool guy's name?"

"Marc Neeson."

"Got it!" Katrina told her, as she headed to see him, hoping he would be as good as the previous swimming pool service technician, Wendy Holokai, who retired and relocated to the Big Island of Hawaii to live with her daughter.

When she got to the swimming pool, the man had his back turned to Katrina, as he was studying the pool. Only after she called out to him, "Mr. Neeson," did he turn around. Her pulse raced in that moment as, at first glance, all Katrina could see was her stalker. Only instead of being clad in a moss-colored Henley T-shirt, denim jeans and high-top black sneakers, he was wearing a chocolate brown uniform. His thick sable hair was in a quiff cut and he had rock and roll–type sideburns. "You—" she stammered.

He cocked a thick brow above solid blue eyes. "Excuse me…"

"What do you want with me?" Katrina demanded, taking a step backward and wondering if she should scream, assuming he meant her harm.

He looked taken aback. "Only to make sure your swimming pool is up to standards for safe and fun use," he insisted. Then, studying her, he asked questioningly, "Is that what you meant?"

Just as she was about to hightail it out of the pool area, Katrina took a second hard look at Marc Neeson. She realized that though he bore some resemblance, her stalker was actually a little taller, more muscular and wore his hair a different way. *It's not the same guy*, she told herself, red-faced. She regretted jumping the gun.

"Yes, of course," she pivoted, and forced a smile. "I'm Katrina Sizemore."

"Marc Neeson, at your service." He stuck out a

friendly narrow hand and she shook it. "Great place you have here."

"Mahalo."

"I can just go over the pool maintenance procedures and if you have any questions, I'm happy to answer."

"Sounds like a plan." Katrina wondered how she could have mistaken him for her stalker. Maybe the idea of him still lurking out there somewhere, as if waiting to catch her at her weakest moment, was getting to her more than she cared to admit. Surely, he wasn't so brazen as to try and confront her at the lodge? Or was he no longer a threat now that his allegations about Joseph's death had been debunked by and large? She turned her attention back to the pool tech and his responsibilities in keeping the pool up to snuff for guests.

"His name is Julio," Dex told Agent Lynda Krause as she played with Barnabas in the backyard of the rented cottage. "He may or may not still be on the island. As the one who supplied Joseph Sizemore with illegal drugs, this Julio could have intended to deal Sizemore a lethal dose. Or been working with other drug traffickers that may have wanted him dead for one reason or another, possibly related to using the Maoli Lodge as one of the points around the island for distributing drugs."

"Looks like we need to find Julio," Lynda agreed, holding a red ball that Barnabas tried to bite as she kept it just out of his reach. "We'll put the first name and physical description through the DEA Intelligence Division's database and see if we can come up with a full name in the system and where he might be holed up."

"Good. The sooner we find Julio, the sooner we can see where he fits into the puzzle in our overall investigation." It was just as important to Dex to give Katrina some peace of mind, once and for all, that Sizemore's death was neither murder nor suicide, but actually due to an accidental drowning.

"So, what else have you come up with from the widow?" Lynda looked at him. "Any new leads?"

"Only in reaffirming that she has played no part in any drug trafficking at the lodge," Dex asserted. "Moreover, Joseph Sizemore appears off the hook as well on that front." He explained how Sizemore sold stocks, which had been verified, to put the money into the lodge, with no indication that he used drug money for that purpose. "If he was caught up in anything else, we'll find out. For now, our focus needs to be on the connections between known drug dealers on the island and use of the lodge, if any."

"I'm down with that." She tossed the ball and they watched as Barnabas scurried after it. "We're making progress," she stated. "Even as we speak, Ishikawa is checking out a storage facility near the property that could be used for drug storage and distribution and even stockpiling of illegal weapons as part of the criminal activities."

Dex nodded with interest as the dog came up to him, dropping the ball at his feet. "Barnabas is ready whenever called upon, aren't you, boy?" He barked in agreement.

Lynda laughed. "Someone's getting antsy being cooped up in this cottage and yard."

"Actually, I think he's enjoying this little vacation." Dex picked up the ball, flung it toward the trees and watched Barnabas go after it. "I don't suppose you were able to come up with any DNA or prints from the second note left by Katrina's stalker?"

"Sorry." Lynda shook her head. "Whoever the man is, he's too clever to make it easy to identify him. Has she seen him again? Or been left any more notes?"

"Not that I'm aware of." Dex assumed Katrina wasn't holding back on him. Now that she knew his true identity, he hoped she knew she could trust him to be on her side. As it was, they both needed to try and get out in front of whoever had left the messages. Though he had downplayed the threat, Dex was still concerned that the man might not be through with the cryptic notes and surveillance. The question was why? What was his end game?

"Maybe the unsub is doing this with ulterior motives," Lynda posed, reading his mind.

"Such as?" Dex wondered.

"To help further along the investigation, while remaining incognito to the degree possible."

"You mean an undercover agent who doesn't want

to blow his cover?" Dex rolled his eyes skeptically. "But had no problem throwing me under the bus by exposing me?"

"Yeah, there is that," she conceded. "Maybe he's a drug trafficker who's gone rogue, but still has connections in law enforcement."

"Well, whoever he is, your cover and Ishikawa's still seem to be intact."

"For now." Lynda flexed her hands. "Maybe not forever."

"We all need to remain vigilant," Dex told her. "If he tries anything that can jeopardize this investigation, we have to be ready to act at a moment's notice."

"I hear you," she agreed.

As he contemplated this and keeping Katrina safe and sound, Dex's cell phone rang. He slipped it out of the pocket of his slim fit jeans and saw that the caller was Agent Ishikawa. "Hey," he answered.

"There's been a break in the investigation," Ishikawa said keenly. "A suspect's been taken into custody for the murder of Agent Roxanne Yamamoto."

DEX STARED THROUGH the one-way window into the interrogation room. Detective Clayton Pietz was grilling the suspect, Kenneth Monaghan, thirtysomething and husky, with long blond hair in a rope ponytail and dark eyes. He was dressed in black jeans and a faded gray jersey T-shirt.

"You're in some deep trouble, Monaghan," Pietz

blasted him on the other side of a square metal table. "We know you cut the brake lines on the Toyota Tacoma that DEA Agent Roxanne Yamamoto was driving the night of Saturday, January 7, which led to the vehicle crashing and Agent Yamamoto's death. How do we know this? Because you left behind just enough of a fingerprint on a brake line that we were able to run it through an FBI database and match it with a fingerprint that was already in the system for your prior criminality."

Monaghan squirmed. "That don't prove I killed her," he snapped defiantly.

"Think again!" Pietz knitted his brows. "We have an eyewitness who can place you hovering around the victim's vehicle prior to her entering it for the fatal drive. If that isn't enough, we confiscated a pair of scissors from your house that you foolishly never bothered to throw away and we were able to link them to the cut brake lines. There's no escaping this, Monaghan," the detective said forcefully. "The first-degree murder of a federal law enforcement officer is serious business with serious consequences. Obviously, you didn't decide to do this all on your own. Your best bet, if you know what's good for you, is to come clean and tell us who put you up to it. Your call…"

Dex groaned within, wondering if the suspect would realize that the hole he'd dug for himself was one he couldn't possibly hope to climb out of. Or was he more frightened by the drug traffickers involved and therefore wouldn't crack? It pained Dex to think that he was looking at the perp responsible for taking away Roxanne's life. He deserved no less. Putting him away for the rest of his miserable life would be anything but a picnic while behind bars, nevertheless. Assuming he didn't cut a deal that gave him some daylight at the end of the tunnel.

"Yeah, I cut the brake lines," Monaghan admitted, head down. "A clean cut."

Pietz leaned forward. "Who hired you to kill her?"

"I don't know. Not exactly." Monaghan drew a long breath. "I was offered twenty grand to slice the brake lines. I only spoke to the guy over the phone," he insisted.

"How did you get the money?" Pietz asked, his voice soaked with skepticism.

"It was left for me in a garbage can in the park," Monaghan claimed.

"What park?"

"Hā'ena State Park." Monaghan's shoulders slumped. "I went right where I was told, found the cash in a brown paper bag and took it. Never heard from the guy again."

Dex couldn't decide if the perp was telling the truth or not. His instincts told him that someone else was calling the shots. But who? When had Roxanne's cover been blown and who ordered the hit on her? Could Katrina's stalker be involved in her murder? Was there any way for the DEA agent to convey what damning information she had come up with from the grave?

He had been so caught up in his thoughts that Dex failed to notice Katrina had come into the room. How long had she been standing there? He had requested that she come in and take a good look at the suspect and see if he had any connection whatsoever to the lodge or any of its employees. Or would being there and observing someone who had confessed to cutting the brake lines of Roxanne's car only unnerve Katrina that much more, given the women's workplace association and Katrina's fragility in coming to terms with her husband's untimely death?

WHEN DEX HAD given her the news that someone had been arrested for Roxanne's murder, Katrina was elated. The fact that she had been an undercover DEA agent did not take away from the friendship they developed during the short time Katrina knew her as Roxanne Kitaoka. Roxanne's heart was in the right place in trying to do her part to rid the island of illicit drugs and those who profited from the trafficking of them. Now Katrina was at the Kauai Police Department, at Dex's request, to see if she recognized the suspect. She jumped at the opportunity that included a squad car to take her there, temporarily leaving the lodge in the more than capable hands of her second in command, Alyson Tennison, to run the ship, in her absence.

Truthfully, Katrina welcomed the chance to shift

her attention away from the embarrassing case of mistaken identity she had with the pool service technician. Turned out he wasn't her stalker after all. Maybe he was gone from her life for good, along with his disturbing notes, his pathetic attempt to play with her head. It was up to her to not allow him to get to her, especially in the face of the evidence that proved Joseph's death an unfortunate accident, notwithstanding his use of meth and fentanyl at the time, ill-fated as it was.

But Roxanne's accident had been ruled a homicide and Katrina gazed through the one-way window at the man suspected of cutting her brake lines—the same man who commanded Dex's attention in that moment, in mourning the death of his DEA colleague. So absorbed was Dex, that he'd failed to look her way when she entered the viewing room. Not that she could blame him, as she understood that whatever feelings he may have developed for her, his priority had to be seeking justice for Agent Yamamoto and tying her death to the drug-trafficking investigation underway on Kauai. Along with the possibilities that its reach could extend to Maoli Lodge.

Running her fingers the length of her long and low ponytail, Katrina cleared her throat to get Dex's attention. He gave her an apologetic crooked grin and said, "Hey. Thanks for coming…"

"Happy to help." She flashed him a thin smile and turned to the window, where she saw Detective Pietz—who had interviewed her shortly after Roxanne's death—interrogating the male suspect. "That him?" she asked.

"Yeah," Dex confirmed. "Name's Kenneth Monaghan. Do you recognize him?"

Katrina zeroed in again on the suspect, studying his face to be sure, before turning back to Dex. "Yes, I do. Two months ago, Kenneth Monaghan was employed by me as a maintenance worker." She paused. "I was forced to fire him after a guest claimed she caught him in the act of stealing items from her room. He tried to deny it, but the jewelry was found among his belongings."

"Did you or the guest press charges?"

"I wanted to," Katrina stressed, "but the guest, content to get back all that was stolen, declined the offer to report it to the police. Apparently, she felt it would take too much time and effort away from making the most of the rest of her vacation."

Dex nodded understandingly and peered at the suspect. "Interesting connection between Monaghan and the Maoli Lodge, nonetheless."

"Do you think he was holding a grudge for being fired," she said with a gasp, "and went after Roxanne in retaliation?" The thought that she might have been responsible for her death unnerved Katrina.

"I seriously doubt one thing had anything to do with the other." Dex set his jaw. "This wasn't about you, Katrina. Without getting into it too deeply, Monaghan was hired to cut the brake lines of Agent Yamamoto's vehicle by someone who wanted to stop her investigation into drug trafficking. Instead, it only emboldened us to work harder to stop the flow of illicit drugs on the island and bring those responsible to justice."

Katrina gulped musingly, putting aside her relief that her actions in firing Kenneth had not cost Roxanne her life. "Do you think whoever was responsible for Roxanne's death was in any way connected to the lodge?" She dreaded to ask.

Dex hunched a shoulder. "No way to know for sure at this point," he said. "My guess is that the drug kingpin has a long reach that spans the island and crosses over to the mainland." He rested a hand on her shoulder, which seemed to penetrate to her very bones. "Whatever the case, Katrina, I'm confident that if anyone associated with the lodge is involved in this, we'll flush out without any of it coming back on you."

"Mahalo, Dex." She took solace with that reassurance, even as Katrina felt a tenseness that told her this still needed to play out like a theater production. Until then, she had to be patient and allow the investigation to run its course. And allow Dex the access he needed in her world until such time, if not beyond.

She gazed into the one-way window and saw the suspect being led out of the room in handcuffs; followed by Detective Pietz, who came inside the viewing room alone. "We've got him," he declared, eyeing Dex.

"Looks that way." Dex met his gaze. "Good work in tracking down Monaghan."

"It was a team effort, Adair." Pietz made a modest expression. "We all wanted to get the person who took out Agent Yamamoto. And we won't stop till the mastermind is brought to justice and anyone else involved in her murder and the drug-trafficking ring."

"Good." Dex stiffened and turned to Katrina.

But before he could say something, Pietz stepped toward her and said evenly, "Mrs. Sizemore, I appreciate your continued cooperation in the investigation."

Katrina smiled. "You can count on me to do whatever I can to further it along in relation to my lodge."

He nodded. "I'll keep that in mind."

Dex informed him that Kenneth Monaghan had once worked at the Maoli Lodge before being terminated. Though Pietz seemed mildly intrigued, he gave that information little weight in the case being built against Monaghan. The murder suspect was to be turned over to the feds for further interrogation and prosecution for the murder of DEA agent Roxanne Yamamoto.

Chapter Ten

"Have you eaten yet?" Dex asked Katrina after they got into his car to take her back to the lodge. He wasn't sure if he was asking her out on a date spontaneously or because he was hungry himself and preferred not to eat alone. Either way, he welcomed a respite from the grind of a DEA investigation.

"No," she said swiftly, adding, "in fact, I'm starving."

"Me too." He grinned at her coolly. "Can I buy you dinner?"

"Yes, I'd love that. But as an island resident, I think it's more appropriate and hospitable that I spring for the meal since you're a visitor—even if you're here on official business…"

Dex wasn't sure whether to be flattered or hold out on paying for the dinner as the right thing to do. Particularly considering that he had invited her. Not the other way around. On the other hand, he was in her neck of the woods, and as such, he wasn't about to argue when all he truly wanted was the chance to spend some personal time with her. What difference did it make who foot the bill? "You're on," he said with genuine enthusiasm.

"Perfect." Her teeth shone. "Where did you have in mind?"

"Anywhere you like," he told her. "I'm game to try anything."

"All right. In that case, I know a great little steak house with a Hawaiian flare on Kiahuna Plantation Drive in the Poipu Shopping Village."

Dex smiled. "Sounds good to me." He followed her directions in getting there and they went inside, taking a seat in a booth. They were handed menus.

"See anything you like?" Katrina asked curiously.

Looking over the menu, from where he sat, Dex couldn't imagine anything more appetizing than the woman across from him. Forcing himself to study the food choices, he saw any number of things that sounded tasty. In the end, he decided to live dangerously insofar as taking a chance on food choices he may not be used to. "Why don't you surprise me with something that tickles your own taste buds," he challenged her.

"I can do that." She curved her nice lips upward in accepting the challenge. "Let's see…"

Katrina ordered them both the filet mignon with red wine sauce, steamed white rice, creamed spinach and Hawaiian herbal tea. She suggested they could try the coconut cheesecake for dessert and Dex was all in.

"So, Dex, you know a lot about me, but I actually know very little about you," Katrina said twenty minutes later, digging her fork into the steamed rice.

He couldn't deny that he had not delved too much into his life for obvious reasons. But now he wanted to share and share alike with the lodge owner. "What would you like to know?" he asked, slicing into the tender filet mignon.

"Well, aside from being a DEA agent with a cover backstory, never married and currently single, I don't suppose you have any children from that onetime special relationship you mentioned, or any other?" She flushed diffidently. "It happens—"

"That it does," he allowed. "But not to me. No kids."

"Would you like to have a family someday?" she asked. "Or is that not in the cards for you and the type of life you lead?"

She's really putting me on the spot with this, Dex told himself, feeling slightly uncomfortable with it. But not in the way she might think. "Yes, I would love to have a family one day—wife, kids, the whole thing," he stressed freely. "It's definitely in the cards and, if anything, the type of life I lead makes me want the stability family brings all the more."

"I see," she murmured, eating her food musingly. He wondered just how much her vision was able to see the full landscape. Being a federal law enforcement officer certainly had its perks and was more than worth his while, but it hardly defined what he truly wanted in life.

Dex gazed at her and asked, curious as well, "What about you? When Joseph was still alive, had you talked about having children?" Dex had little doubt that Katrina would make a great mother, even if she wasn't as sure.

"We talked about it," she said with a maudlin slant to her tone. "The plan was to get established with the lodge and then start a family." Katrina stared down at her plate and back up. "Sometimes plans have a way of blowing up in your face. Or at least thrown entirely off track by fate."

"I understand where you're coming from." Dex sat back, taking a breath. "When I was young, I used to hang out a lot with my older sister, Rita. I thought the world of her and imagined being a doting uncle to her kids when she found someone to love and be loved by. But that didn't happen," he bemoaned. "The man she ended up with was a drug dealer. He got her hooked on heroin. Rita overdosed on the drug… She never lived to reach the age of twenty."

Katrina reacted, reaching a hand across the table to touch his. "I'm so sorry, Dex."

"Yeah, I am too." Their skin connecting did wonders to lessen the sad memories, if not take away the pain altogether. "As you said, sometimes fate steps in the way of what you thought would happen and you just have to deal with it."

She met his eyes. "Was it your sister's death that motivated you to become a DEA agent?"

"That was certainly a factor," he acknowledged. "Along with growing up in Detroit and wanting to do my part to help rid the country of drug addiction and the people who profited from this as drug dealers and the like."

"Which brought you to Kauai and into my life," Katrina pointed out with a sensitive look.

"Yeah." He saw the irony in that, considering this was likely the only way they would have ever crossed paths. And given the fact that this meant something to him, he wouldn't have changed a thing. Other than to have not wanted to see her and the Maoli Lodge dragged into the investigation, causing Katrina burdens she did not need. Dex was glad, nevertheless, that she had been cleared of involvement in any drug-related crimes and he could see her in the right light as someone who captured his attention. Over and beyond being duty bound as a DEA agent.

"Are you up for that coconut cheesecake for dessert?" Katrina broke his reverie, having removed her hand from his.

"Absolutely," he answered smilingly.

As they ate, Katrina leaned toward Dex and asked, "Do you have any plans to settle down anytime soon? Or is your calling as a DEA agent such that you don't see that happening for the foreseeable future?"

If he didn't know better, Dex might almost think

that she was interviewing him to become her husband at some point. Or was he misinterpreting because the idea appealed to him in more ways than he had come to terms with? "I haven't really thought that far ahead," he spoke truthfully. "If I had, I would like to believe that for the right person I would love to settle down to a life together." He allowed that to hang there before continuing. "Regarding my job, I don't really see it as a calling, but rather a privilege to use my education and skills in a productive manner. That said, it doesn't mean I couldn't find other ways to make a meaningful contribution to society…and that special someone who would become the most important reason for waking up every morning."

Katrina's eyes lit with admiration. "Well said."

"Mahalo." Dex thought the Hawaiian word was apropos. He also hoped she took his words for what they were worth, knowing she was just the type of woman he could fall for in a big way and have that kind of life in paradise with. He thought about her earlier confession of no longer being in love with her husband at the time of his death. Dex wondered where things stood between himself and Katrina and if she might be willing to open her heart to someone else. Him. "So, just how bad were things between you and Joseph toward the end?"

Katrina dabbed a napkin at the corner of her generous mouth as she mulled over the question that obviously required some careful thought. "Bad enough to have me questioning if we were truly ever meant to be together," she stated sadly.

"What did you come up with…?" he pressed.

"The reality that the romance in our lives had stalled. Whether it was from the daily grind of running a lodge, or Joseph being consumed with work, play and apparently illicit drug use, we weren't clicking at that point and I think he knew that as much as I did." She sighed plaintively and made a face. "So, if you're asking if I am able to move past my marriage to Joseph if someone new were to enter my life, the answer is yes."

"Good to know." Dex grinned. Her words were music to his ears, and he felt an irregular patter of his heart and its potential for falling in love thereafter. She was clearly of the same mind, even if he was still presently caught up in a drug-trafficking investigation that commanded his attention, whether he preferred that to be the case or not. "Do you want to get out of here?"

Katrina smiled readily. "Yes, I believe I would."

"WOULD YOU LIKE to come in?" she asked as he walked her to her door a little while later. *Please say yes*, Katrina thought, not wanting to appear too eager. But they had waited long enough to act on the sexual vibes that had sizzled between them since practically the very beginning. If Dex should turn her down, Katrina wasn't quite sure how she would take it. Unless she was reading him wrong during the dinner conversation, he was as open to the possibilities for romance as she was. The fact that he was still investigating drug trafficking on the island and even within the boundaries of her property did not preclude them from testing the waters and seeing if there was anything there worth fighting for.

"I'd love to come in," Dex told her, showing his teeth in a handsome smile, warming her heart in the process.

Katrina smiled back, ignoring the butterflies in her stomach as she led him inside. It was the first time since Joseph's death that she had been so inclined to want another man's company. But she believed the timing was right. Or, if not perfect, certainly lent itself to the moment at hand and whatever came of it. "Can I get you something to drink?" she asked, thinking that some wine might be nice about now.

"Sure, whatever you're having," he said, seemingly unable to take his eyes off her.

"Two glasses of wine coming up. Be right back." Katrina left him standing in the great room as she stepped inside the kitchen. She glanced at the wedding band still on her finger since it was first put there by her late husband, and Katrina realized it was time to remove it. The ring that had once been a symbol of love was now merely a piece of jewelry that was no longer apropos for who she was today and the future she wanted to move toward. She twisted it off her finger and quietly put the ring in a drawer. Removing two goblets from the distressed oak cabinet, Katrina set them on the quartz counter-top. From the fridge, she took out an opened bottle of tropical guava wine and half-filled each wineglass. Only when she felt his warm breath on the back of her neck did Katrina realize Dex had come into the kitchen. She faced him, her heart suddenly beating wildly, and handed him a goblet. "For you."

He tasted, allowing the liquid to roll through his mouth. "Excellent."

"You think?" She sipped her own wine, feeling jittery and excited at the same time.

"Yeah." He set his glass on the counter and hers as well. Wrapping his arms around her slender waist and pulling her closer, Dex uttered in a sexy voice, "There's something else I have a taste for even more…"

"Oh really?" Her lashes fluttered with anticipation. "And what might that be?"

"This…" He cupped her face, tilted his head and moved in for a kiss. She reciprocated in kind, feeling its potency from head to toe. They stood there tasting each other's mouths for what seemed like an eternity of unbearable desire, before Dex pried their lips apart. "I don't think I'm telling you anything you don't already know, but I find you to be incredibly attractive, Katrina," he voiced gutturally.

"I could say the same about you, Dex," she uttered with swollen lips, and meant every word. She could only imagine what a specimen he was with his clothes off. "Maybe we should head to the bedroom…"

He gave her another mouthwatering kiss, then looked her in the eye. "You sure you're ready for that?"

If she was any surer, Katrina imagined she would burst. "Yes, I'm sure." Then she held his gaze with uncertainty. "Are you?" she asked.

"Never been more ready," he declared lustfully.

"Neither have I." Katrina couldn't argue with what her body was telling her loud and clear. She wanted him in the worst way. Make that the best way between a man and woman. That was more than enough for her without overthinking it, as she took one more sip of wine and he did the same, before she led him by the hand to her bedroom.

There, Katrina took her hair out of the ponytail, allowing it to hang free and loose. "I love your hair that way," Dex told her and ran a hand through it before cupping her chin and putting their lips together.

"Nice to know," she said, enjoying the feel of his mouth on hers as they kissed passionately, before separating and removing their clothes like they were on fire. As she stood naked, Katrina was surprised at just how relaxed and confident she felt being naked with a man for the first time since Joseph's death. Was she truly ready to make love again? Give away her heart and body? Or was it more who she was about to go to bed with, as she stared at the physical specimen Dex represented. She couldn't remember a time when she was so enamored with and desirous of someone. Whether this was wrong or so very right, her instincts were in overdrive in making this happen.

Forcing her eyes away from Dex, who seemed just as taken by what he saw, she stepped over to a rattan nightstand and took a condom package out of the drawer. "This is for you," she said, handing it to him.

He accepted it without preface and, in practically a blink of an eye, was ready to pick up where they left off. And so much more. Effortlessly. Dex lifted Katrina off her feet and carried her to the driftwood queen low bed, where he pulled down the quilted ivory bedspread and laid her on the soft pomegranate-colored sateen sheets. Sliding next to her, he wasted little time in using his big hands and nimble fingers to caress Katrina's breasts and body expertly, sending waves of delight throughout her. By the time he kissed her again, she was more than ready to move to the next stage of lovemaking. "Take me, Dex," she murmured, reaching out and pulling him toward her. "Please. Now!"

"Believe me, it would be my pleasure," he voiced thickly. "Make that *our* pleasure, by the time we're through!" He made his way between her legs and she urgently guided him inside. As though a tidal wave of unbridled desire were unleashed, their bodies came together wildly, and Katrina found herself unable to hold back from climaxing almost immediately. How did it happen so soon? She tried to recall when this had ever occurred during her marriage. Sadly, no memories surfaced. Was it simply not as good previously? Her focus returned to the moment at hand with her legs wrapped securely around Dex's firm back, holding on for dear life as the powerful sensations paralyzed her with pleasure.

Only when she came back down from the incredible high, did Katrina know that it was but the opening salvo of an experience that she embraced wholeheartedly. She wanted to feel the joy of their mutual orgasm and suspected it would be even more earth-shattering. "Your turn," she murmured selflessly to her lover.

"Our turn together," Dex countered urgently, as he kissed her and picked up the pace. With staying power that amazed Katrina, she arched her back and met him halfway every time, their hunger-driven gazes locked on to one another unblinkingly. The primeval urges took over Katrina like never before and she didn't question her need. Or his, as the fan overhead did nothing to lessen the soaring temperatures in the bedroom while they made love. She felt Dex's trembling body and ragged breaths, as the level of intensity soared higher and higher and their rhythmical heartbeats fell in total sync.

By the time it was over, Katrina breathlessly rode the wave of pure sexual delight for as long as it carried her lithe, moist body, while clinging to Dex in the aftermath. Only then did she wonder where they would go from there. Or had this incredible journey in the face of a drug-trafficking and murder investigation already run its course?

"This doesn't have to mean anything," Katrina found herself saying, feeling the need to not put any pressure or expectations on the man she had just made love to. No matter her own thoughts on the subject, which based on the ardent way she'd reacted to him, pretty much spoke for itself. Didn't it?

Chapter Eleven

"But it does mean something," Dex said with more than a little assurance, his voice unwavering and his arms holding Katrina up against his body. He had just engaged in mind-blowing sex with arguably the most beautiful woman he'd ever seen. Or, at the very least, had the pleasure of getting to know in the biblical sense. To suggest it meant nothing would indicate that the last hour of all-consuming intimacy was merely a flash in the pan. A simple sexual release void of any emotional attachment. He wasn't wired that way. Not in the slightest. Not with her. And the incredibly seductive sounds she made and her sensual body movements during their lovemaking told him that it was much more than just casual sex for her too. Dex suspected that her statement was more of a defense mechanism than anything, to avoid getting hurt. This was something he would never do to her willfully. Especially not after their succumbing to a mutual attraction, leaving him wanting so much more.

"And just what is that something?" Katrina challenged him, with a silky-smooth leg draped invitingly over his. "Or do you even know?"

Dex touched her flushed cheek. "I know that what we just did was amazing," he spoke sincerely. More than he could ever have imagined when handed this assignment. "We're good together, Katrina. There's no denying that."

"I'm not denying it," she promised him. "But that's the problem, isn't it? I'm a widow, operating a lodge on Kauai. You have an entirely different life going on. With the demands of your profession as a DEA agent, I'm not sure I'm cut out for a 'whenever we can get together but are otherwise apart' type relationship."

"Neither am I," he confessed, never expecting to meet someone who could be the woman of his dreams. But he had and he didn't want to see her slip away. How could he prevent it and maintain the unpredictable life on the go that he had become accustomed to in combatting drug-related criminality in the United States and beyond? "I care for you," Dex told her, locking eyes with Katrina so she knew how serious he was.

"I care for you too, Dex." She rested her head on his shoulder. "But is that enough for either of us?"

It was certainly a good place to start, Dex believed. That was enough to give him hope of a future with Katrina. "We'll figure it out," he promised.

She nodded, seemingly content in that thought.

But for how long? Dex knew it was on him to make it work and he fully intended to. He lifted her chin and kissed Katrina on the mouth. The kiss lingered for a while, with both of them into it, before he reluctantly pulled back. "Hate to kiss and run, but I need to check on Barnabas."

"Of course." She licked her lips. "He's probably wondering where you've been."

Dex chuckled. "Yeah, he does tend to get a bit antsy when we're apart too long."

"I can only imagine," she uttered teasingly.

"Me too." He hadn't even left and Dex was already starting to miss her company. The thought of them being apart too long was excruciating. But duty called. He kissed Katrina's soft shoulder and rolled off the bed, enjoying the view of her lying there naked tantalizingly. "Stay there," he said. "I can see myself out."

Dex quickly dressed and pushed aside his hesitancy to leave, knowing he had no choice. "Catch you later," he told Katrina and gave her a goodbye kiss, as she remained in bed, covered up but smiling to let him know the door was open. All he had to do was be willing to meet her halfway. It seemed more than reasonable to him, once he got past the current investigation that included keeping her safe.

THE MOMENT HE stepped inside the cottage, Dex knew something was wrong. The place had been ransacked as if it had been hit by a tornado. His first thought was Barnabas. Was he hurt? Was the intruder, or in-truders, still there? Immediately, Dex removed his DEA-issued and loaded 40 caliber Glock 27 pistol from a concealed carry holster. He had taken the lib-erty of arming himself routinely, after leaving the firearm locked in his glove compartment while visit-ing Katrina. Moving cautiously through the cottage, he checked each room, nook and cranny, and saw no sign of anyone. What the hell were they looking for? He considered that this was where Roxanne was staying. Did the break-in have anything to do with her undercover assignment, which he had inherited?

Dex kept the gun in a ready-to-use position as he went to the back door. His heart was racing in fear of what he might find in the backyard, where he had left Barnabas for some exercise. The thought that someone had harmed—or perhaps killed—his canine best friend nearly broke Dex. He opened the door, expecting either the worst or to come face-to-face with an armed assailant, instead there was only Barnabas standing there on all four feet with seem-ingly not a care in the world, while showing no signs of being injured. Dex nearly jumped for joy and, after determining that there was no one hiding amongst the fruit trees, embraced the K-9 dog. "Good to see you're safe and sound, boy!" Barnabas demonstrated mutual affection by licking his hands and face. "You wait out here and I'll get you something to eat and finish checking out the place."

The K-9 cop seemed reluctant to remain in the

backyard, but obeyed, as Dex wanted to get a fo-
rensic team in there to see what they could come up
with, if anything. The fact that someone was willing
to boldly encroach on his space told him that they
must be closing in on the drug traffickers and others
with a stake in the game. And they were willing to
do whatever they needed to get what they wanted.
No matter who got in their way. Well, as far as Dex
was concerned, this was hardly going to deter the
Task Force from going after those who were committing offenses on Kauai soil, including murder.
He left Barnabas to himself, while Dex went back
inside and got on the cell phone, first calling Lynda
and Ishikawa, then Clayton Pietz and some other
members of the Task Force, to inform them of the
break-in.

Thirty minutes later, Dex was being interviewed
by Detective Sergeant Vera Tolentino of the Kauai
PD's Property Crimes Unit. In her early thirties, she
was of medium height and build, with brunette hair
in an A-line cut, and light brown eyes. "Is there anything missing that you know of, Agent Adair?"

Dex considered the mess left behind, but couldn't
actually say anything of note was missing. "Doesn't
look like they took anything of value," he admitted,
while knowing that as a precautionary measure—
given the disappearance of key items from Roxanne's
belongings upon her death—he had taken the liberty
of keeping his cell phone, laptop and two firearms on

his person or locked inside the car whenever away from the cottage.

"Lucky you," Vera remarked, as they stood in the main room. "Lately, there's been a number of burglaries in the Koloa area. Mostly teenagers looking to grab anything they can steal to pay for drugs or just to pass the time out of plain boredom. Apparently, from what you're telling me, they came away from here empty-handed."

"Not sure this was a simple case of burglary." Dex almost hated to tell her, even if she made a good argument on that front.

She flashed him a suspicious stare. "What aren't you telling me?"

Sticking to the need-to-know basis for information, he responded evasively, "Let's just say that with a major drug-trafficking operation underway on the island, there are more than burglars who may have wanted to hit the place in a bad way."

"I see." She made a note of this. "Well, our crime scene investigators will be here shortly to collect any evidence they can find. We'll be sure to coordinate our efforts with the vice section and you guys and go from there."

"Sounds good." Dex smiled at her and watched briefly as she got on her cell phone. Ten minutes later, he was conferring with Lynda, Ishikawa and Clayton Pietz on the mysteries of the break-in. None of them were quite certain what—or who—was be-

hind it. They all seemed to rule out the burglary
angle on the whole.

Detective Pietz drew his brows together. "Your
cottage being ransacked so soon after we nailed Kenneth Monaghan does appear to be more than coincidence."

"Yeah, I was thinking the same thing." Dex con-
curred in connecting the dots between their investigation and his role in the scheme of things. Including
working with Katrina to weed out potential perpetrators and unsubs. Could her firing Monaghan just
before he cut the brake lines of Roxanne's car be
a factor in her onetime cottage being burglarized?
Was that something that could still put Katrina in
jeopardy?

"So, you think this is something akin to a warning shot to say we're on to you and the probe into
drug trafficking?" Ishikawa questioned.

"It's possible," Dex conceded, thinking about Katrina's still unidentified stalker, whose motivation
and insinuations remained a mystery. "It's just as
likely that whoever killed Roxanne had figured out
our connection and were still looking for something
she left behind. Or at least they believed that to be
the case."

"I think that's a bit of a stretch," Lynda chimed
in, standing flat-footed. "If they didn't find it after
she was killed, there's no reason to believe she would
have passed the torch to you, so to speak, and you

would be dumb enough to leave it hanging around for them to find."

"Good point as well," Dex said, thoughtful. "But here's the thing. My cover has been blown…and likely my trusty and thankfully unharmed K-9 companion's as well. At least in the eyes of someone. And I'm staying at the same place where Agent Yamamoto had ample time to collect and hide evidence. Maybe it's still here somewhere and can bring down the entire illicit drug operation, if found. We need to keep all options on the table as we try to get to the root of it."

"I agree," Pietz said. "The people we're dealing with mean business. They'll stop at nothing to keep their profitable trafficking of drugs going. That includes sending a message to any of us involved in the criminal investigation, whether it's a warning shot, as Ishikawa put it, or an all-out war. We need to be ready for whatever comes next and come back twice as hard."

"We're with you, Pietz," Lynda declared, and Dex didn't argue against it. They did need to remain united as a Task Force in fighting a common enemy. One that he feared still potentially placed Katrina and her lodge in the line of fire.

KATRINA WAS STILL riding high on the explosive sex with Dex, if not the uncertainty of where this might carry them for the future. *We'll figure it out*, she replayed in her head what he'd said in that respect.

Would they? Or were they really just fooling themselves that it could work? Yes, they were great in bed and had hit it off. But could they truly bridge the gap between a mainlander who worked on dangerous missions for the Drug Enforcement Administration and a widowed owner of a lodge on a relatively peaceful Hawaiian island?

I can't allow myself to get too carried away after one night in bed, incredible as it was, Katrina thought, having put her clothes back on and made herself a cup of coconut coffee. What would be, would be. She needed to keep a proper perspective and refrain from putting too much pressure on Dex or herself in wanting to make this work between them. Perhaps once he had put his current investigation into drug trafficking in the case closed category, they could sit down and talk about what they envisioned in a real relationship and see if the two measured up. In the meantime, as a single, healthy woman with needs like everyone else, there was no harm in enjoying Dex's company for as long as they both saw eye to eye regarding spending time together, and go from there.

Her ruminations were halted as Katrina became aware of the knock on her door. Though she was technically off duty, the dictates of operating a lodge successfully required her to be on call at all times for anything that came up. What was it this time? A leaking sink? Overflowing tub? A belligerent or inebriated guest? Katrina prepared herself for any possibility as she padded in her bare feet across the floor to the door and opened it. To her joyous surprise, standing there was Dex. Along with Barnabas.

"Hey," she said demurely, eyeing the DEA agent curiously. "Didn't expect to see you again so soon."

"Barnabas and I need a place to crash for the night," Dex said tonelessly, adding, "he's perfectly housetrained."

"Of course, you're welcome to stay for as long as you like." Katrina smiled and welcomed them inside. She didn't feel at all as though her offer was being too generous, because she had plenty of room. She doubted Dex would ever take her up on it, so long as they hadn't made a firm commitment to each other. Only then did she gaze at him and ask nervously, "What happened?"

Dex grimaced. "My cottage was vandalized," he voiced angrily.

"What?" Her eyes popped wide. "By who?"

"We're still trying to determine that. The police department seems to think it was just some locals looking for money to buy drugs. Or to wreck the place just for the hell of it."

"But you don't believe that," she deduced.

He gazed down at his dark loafers and back up. "If I had to hazard a guess, I'd say someone broke in looking for something connected to the drug-trafficking case."

She glanced at Barnabas, who had moved quietly into a corner and seemed totally disinterested in the conversation. "That would mean whoever was behind it had to know you're a DEA agent."

"Or that Roxanne was and had stayed there before me. Either way, it's definitely suspicious in nature."

Katrina's heart dropped. "Are we talking about maybe the stalker who warned me about not trusting you?" she asked with dread.

Dex's jaw tensed. "Not necessarily," he said. "He would certainly be a suspect. But the people trafficking drugs in and around the island have more than one way to come at you. Whoever got Kenneth Monaghan to do their dirty work in killing Agent Roxanne Yamamoto could've easily figured out that she might have a replacement and made it their business to determine who it was."

Katrina knew he was also trying to tell her it had nothing to do with their involvement, per se. Or even her own association with both Roxanne and, of course, Joseph, as his widow. Yet Katrina still got a chill in believing that the danger was all around them and the perpetrators would not stop as long as whoever was calling the shots felt confidently above the law.

Before she knew it, Dex had wrapped his arms around her. "It'll be all right." He spoke with a mixture of softness and sureness. "For both of us. I promise."

"You think?" She lifted her chin at him.

"Yeah, I do." He took a breath and held her a little tighter.

Katrina leaned against his hard body, taking in his words and what she took as a dual meaning that they would both get past the current dangerous environment and also be okay in their own future. She embraced both concepts, while still being concerned about what it all meant.

Chapter Twelve

Katrina was restless as she slept through the rainy night, despite being held snugly for much of it by Dex. She had a frightening dream about coming face-to-face with her stalker, only to have him lunge at her with a long-bladed supersharp knife. The type one could imagine Jack the Ripper used to carve up his victims. Just as she screamed, Katrina snapped open her eyes and heard only a low hum coming from her mouth. It was only a nightmare. The first she could remember that involved the mystery man who had left her notes and followed her around at least once.

As she regained her bearings, Katrina turned around, expecting to find Dex sound asleep. Instead, his side of the bed was empty. Feeling slightly disappointed, she dragged herself up, wondering if he had made breakfast or at least coffee. Slipping into a short kimono robe, she left the room and went into the kitchen. No Dex. Or even Barnabas. Did she drive them away? After not finding a note, Katrina checked her cell phone for messages. There was a text from Dex that told her he had gotten up early to give Barnabas some exercise and then both would need to get back to work. He asked that she keep him informed if she ran into any problems. That was code to Katrina for possibly whoever ransacked his cottage. Or perhaps if she spotted the man who had stalked her.

Dex ended the text message with the words, Miss you. Katrina missed him too. Maybe more than she was willing to admit to him, if not herself. Wherever this was going, she still needed to remain grounded and remember that the lodge needed to be her first priority at the moment. Just as Dex had an ongoing investigation that he had to focus on if they were ever to get past it. Asking him to push that aside, or to the back burner and instead explore their budding romance, wouldn't be fair to either of them. Especially not when drug-related criminals were still within their midst and apparently as dangerous as ever.

Twenty minutes later, Katrina was in her office, working. In fact, business had been brisk of late, with bookings going through the roof for this time of year and few empty rooms for the foreseeable future. It looked as though they were finally beginning to turn the corner in becoming profitable, in spite of Joseph's mismanagement before he died. *I certainly can't take anything for granted*, she told herself, knowing that you got what you put into it. Beyond that, to keep the lodge running smoothly, it needed to continue to be a go-to resort location in the ever-competitive town of Poipu on the island's south shore. Katrina understood that for her long-term survival in the hospitality business, the Maoli Lodge had to get past the drug-trafficking probe once and for all.

"Hey, I've been looking for you," Alyson said, stepping inside the room and snapping Katrina from her musings.

"You found me." She smiled at the assistant manager. "What's up?"

"Just a scheduling conflict with a housekeeper. Apparently, Sophie had a little too much to drink last night and overslept."

"Oh dear." Katrina made a face. Sophie Fernandez was one of their recent hires. What she lacked in experience, she more than made up for with hard work. Till now.

"Fear not, I took care of it," Alyson stated proudly. "Did a little rearranging of schedules so she could come in later without a single room needing to be delayed for cleaning."

Katrina's eyes lit with gratitude. "What would I ever do without you?"

"You'd manage just fine," she insisted, downplaying her role in keeping things running as smoothly as possible. "I'm happy to be your right hand in making sure things don't fall apart."

"And I'm just as happy to have you around, believe me." Katrina couldn't help but think about someone who was no longer around, Roxanne Yamamoto. Though she'd been only using her position with housekeeping to investigate the lodge, Katrina sincerely believed the DEA agent was a good person and obviously good at her job. She would have loved to have gotten to know Roxanne better. But she would never have that chance, as fate had intervened in the cruelest way. At least the man responsible for her brakes failing had been brought to justice and would pay the price. Katrina could only wonder how many more heads would roll before this was fully over.

"So, I noticed you've been spending time lately with the piano man." Alyson again cut into her thoughts.

Katrina blushed. "You're right," she admitted. She saw no reason to deny it, even if she had to maintain Dex's cover for as long as he needed her to. "We sort of hit it off."

"Figured as much." Alyson flashed her teeth. "Good for you. I know you loved Joseph, but you're allowed to move on at some point. Now seems to be as good a time as any."

"I agree." Katrina welcomed her support. Getting past Joseph's passing was not going to be easy. But she had a right to meet someone else with whom she could find a rapport and fall in love. *Did I just say fall in love?* Katrina asked herself in shock at the suddenness of the emotion toward a man she had not known for very long. But then again, she had known Joseph for a while before they became an item. As it turned out, in many ways she had not known him at all. And if the truth be told, may never have really been in love, so much as liking the idea of love. Not the way she was beginning to feel about Dex. Could he feel the same way about her? Or did he need more time—and even distance—to come to terms with what she meant to him? "We'll see how it goes," she tossed out, as if what they had was strictly casual. It wasn't to her anyway.

"At least he has some musical talent to keep you going," Alyson said with a chuckle. "Wish I could say that about the men I've been dating lately."

Katrina laughed. "Well, there is that." She was amazed Dex found the time to keep up with the piano playing, given his day job. Admittedly, having such a skill was a great cover for someone working undercover.

"Being a private investigator to boot probably doesn't hurt the cause either," Alyson joked, moving over to her desk. "Never know when you might need someone to do a little digging for you."

"That's true too." Katrina thought it wise to move away from this conversation, knowing that Dex was doing digging that went well beyond her needs. "Anyway, let's talk about the hula dancers we have coming in to perform in the Kahiko Lounge this weekend…"

WITH BARNABAS ON a leash and behaving himself, Dex walked around the lodge, allowing the dog to stretch his legs and see if he picked up any signs of drugs. Though Katrina wasn't a suspect any longer, there was still the possibility that the lodge was being used by traffickers to facilitate their agenda. Particularly considering that someone had the gall to break into his rented cottage, suggesting that the connection was there. It irked him that this was putting Katrina at risk, especially as he was trying his best to lessen the threat to her health and well-being. Now that they had moved their relationship up a notch—make that a few notches—he wasn't about to let the bad guys rain on their parade and prevent more sunshine between him and Katrina on Kauai. Or anywhere else they could get closer.

Dex went outside to allow Barnabas to do his thing in a cluster of bushes, while barely noticing a bakery delivery truck parked out front. He didn't have much of a sweet tooth, though he was definitely becoming sweet on Katrina, who was much more to his liking as a delicacy. Besides his delight in spending the night together, getting little sleep in the process, she was everything he'd ever wanted in a woman and partner to build a life with. And, yes, to fall in love with. What was not to love in the beautiful, intelligent and successful businesswoman? Dex wasn't about to shy away from the type of life he could have with Katrina. She seemed amenable to the possibilities, which thrilled him even more. Once the investigation was over, he looked forward to having a conversation with her about a future and, hopefully, find a way to make this work between them. No matter the obstacles that might present themselves, given their different lots in life.

Back inside, Dex was sure Katrina was up and at it, meaning no chance for any morning delight. What about the afternoon to have a repeat performance of last night? He found himself inside the Kahiko Lounge, which was mostly empty at this time of day. Dex didn't spot Gordon, but the head bartender was never far away, and seemed to have his eye on one of the daytime waitresses. Dex drifted toward the piano. He wasn't scheduled to play today, but felt the spirit move him in doing a song or two as a freebie and for practice. Sitting on the bench, he freed Barnabas from the leash, which the dog clearly welcomed as he curled up silently beside Dex, seemingly ready to snooze.

Dex started playing "Hawaiian Lullaby," and was about halfway through the popular song, when Barnabas stood up and shot across the lounge. He wound up near the bar and seemed attracted to something atop it. The dog had been trained to react this way in the presence of drugs. Dex's own radar activated. *What have you latched upon, boy?* He took his fingers off the piano keys and headed over to see for himself.

Approaching the bar, Dex spotted the sheet cake on the counter. Jumping up at it, but just out of his reach, Barnabas only settled down when Dex reached the dog and kept him at bay. "What do we have here?" Dex asked out loud as he studied the rectangular cake in a baking pan with a see-through plastic lid. Grabbing a napkin off the counter, he carefully lifted a corner of the lid until it gave and came off in its entirety. Setting it aside, he saw a layer of coffee grounds. He dug into and lifted up a cellophane wrapped package. Putting it up to his nose, Dex smelled a mixture of a flowery and chemical scent that he recognized. There were several other packages hidden as well. The coffee sheet cake was a clever front for what Dex knew to be several pounds of cocaine. What the hell was it doing there?

"Good job, Barnabas," he praised the dog, while continuing to study the illicit finding. "I'll take it from here." The drug-sniffing canine seemed content at that point to wait for further instructions.

When Gordon Guerrero came from the back room carrying a case of wine, he saw Dex and said nonchalantly, "Hey."

"Where did this come from?" Dex glanced at the disguised cake and back at the bartender with a hard gaze.

"Why do you ask?" He set the wine down and took note of Barnabas suddenly growling at him as though the enemy. "And what's with your dog?"

Dex realized now was the time to end the charade and come clean. Either Gordon Guerrero would prove to be an asset. Or a drug trafficker. What came next would determine whether to solicit his help. Or place him under arrest. Removing his badge, Dex flashed it in the face of the potential suspect. "DEA Special Agent Adair," he announced firmly. "And this is Barnabas, my narcotic detection K-9."

Gordon's mouth dropped. He looked ill at ease. "Does Katrina know…?"

"Yes, she knows." Dex didn't beat around the bush. He was glad that Katrina had kept his cover under wraps. But the moment had come when everything was about to be out on the table. "Let's get back to the cake," he said sharply. "Who brought it here?"

"A woman from the bakery delivered it," Gordon claimed. "Said it was for a guest's birthday. We have birthdays, graduations, weddings, you-name-it events at the lodge all the time."

Dex recollected the bakery delivery truck outside. He must have just missed getting a look at the driver. "I need to know everything you can tell me about the delivery woman."

Gordon peered at him inquisitively. "You wanna tell me what this is all about, Agent Adair?"

Dex held his gaze. "The cake is actually made of cocaine."

"Seriously?"

"Do you see me laughing?" Dex's mouth was decidedly downturned at the corners. "Who is the cake of cocaine for?"

"The woman said his name was Julio," Gordon responded succinctly.

Julio. The name immediately rang a bell in Dex's head like a fire alarm, as he recalled that a Julio was the drug dealer Larry Nakanishi said gave Joseph Sizemore the meth. Dex was all but certain that the unsub also supplied Katrina's late husband with synthetic fentanyl and that he and the man slated to receive the cocaine cake was, in fact, one and the same. "When is Julio supposed to pick up the birthday cake?" Dex asked.

Gordon glanced at his watch. "She said he would come and get it at noon."

Dex got out his cell phone and noted that was more than an hour away. Not much time to operate, but enough. He regarded the bartender and stated in earnest, "I'm giving you the benefit of the doubt, for Katrina's sake, that you're not caught up in this, Guerrero."

"I'm not," he insisted with a strained look of innocence. "If someone is dealing drugs at the lodge, I want to help bring 'em down."

Dex's instincts told him the man was on the level. "You can start by describing the delivery woman," he told him. "Then we'll need your cooperation as we set up a sting to go after the dealers..."

"You've got it." Gordon said convincingly, as Barnabas kept his eyes glued to him. "The woman was Hawaiian, I think, maybe in her late twenties, slim, and had long dark hair that was tied up in the back." He sighed. "I wasn't exactly checking her out, so can't give you much more than that."

"It's enough," Dex assured him. The description would give them something to work with.

He stepped away from the bartender and called Ishikawa and Lynda with the latest and unexpected turn of events in their investigation. Then he got Pietz on the line to help set things in motion for what they hoped would be an all-important step in taking down a drug-trafficking organization on Kauai.

Then came the hard part for Dex. He needed to inform Katrina that the Maoli Lodge was being used to camouflage and transport cocaine in the form of a sheet cake. And worse, one of the suspects they hoped to nab was very likely the same person who gave illegal drugs to Joseph Sizemore. Which may well have contributed to his death.

Chapter Thirteen

To say she was shocked to learn that four to five pounds of cocaine had been brought to the lodge disguised as a cake would be an understatement. Katrina was sickened when Dex delivered the news, having pulled her to the side just when she had gone looking for him and Barnabas after they had left her suite this morning without waking her to say good-bye. Their investigation involving the Maoli Lodge had brought them to this point and she would have to deal with it. Including the fact that the cocaine had reportedly been left for a man named Julio, possibly the same drug dealer Joseph used to get meth and perhaps fentanyl as well. Then there was the re-introduction of Dex's fellow DEA agents, Sylvester Ishikawa and Lynda Krause, whom Katrina knew as lodge guests, Mr. and Mrs. Sylvester Hayashi. According to Dex, the urgency of the situation demanded that the team work out in the open with full disclosure, as it related to her in giving them full cooperation. Katrina welcomed this and completely understood the need for secrecy for as long as was necessary to keep from jeopardizing the investigation. She had to admit that Agents Ishikawa and Krause were convincing as a loving couple, enjoying what was supposed to be a second honeymoon on Kauai. Katrina couldn't help but wonder just how much of the chemistry was the real deal. She considered the strength of the chemistry between her and Dex that had actually strengthened once his own cover had been exposed and she got to know the true man behind the mask.

"We believe the cocaine came from a bakery that may be used as a front for receiving and distributing the stuff," Dex informed her as they stood near a fountain and in between tropical plants. "We're trying to locate the delivery woman, along with the source of the illegal drug operation."

"How long do you think this has been going on?" Katrina dreaded to ask. If she were held liable for being a party to drug trafficking, it would be equally devastating to her business and to her personally.

"Can't say for sure, but my belief is that the traffickers are adept at moving from one location to another in their efforts to minimize risk and maximize profits." Dex lowered his voice a heartening octave. "There is no evidence that this has been a regular occurrence at the lodge. Gordon felt certain that he had never before seen the woman who delivered the cocaine. And I asked the front desk and there's no indication that a Julio ever checked in today or yesterday."

"Maybe he used a fake name." Katrina creased her nose. "Or his real one."

"More likely that he wouldn't have wanted to leave a trail of DNA and fingerprints behind by taking a room," Dex said confidently. "I'm guessing that he only intends to pick up his cocaine and get the hell out of the lodge as quickly and inconspicuously as possible."

Katrina sucked in a deep breath. "So, when is this going to go down?" she asked, having been briefed on the sting he had put into gear.

"Anytime now." Dex put his hands on her shoulders. "We aren't expecting any trouble, but to be on the safe side, I think it's best if you stay in your suite until the operation is complete."

She gazed up at him uneasily. "You really think that's necessary?" He had told her that the plan was to allow Julio to pick up the cocaine cake and leave unscathed, while hoping he would lead them to bigger fish, other players and more evidence of criminal activity in the illicit trade.

"Better safe than sorry." Dex met her eyes warmly. "I've really grown to care for you, Katrina. If anything were to happen to you because of this, I'd never forgive myself."

"I feel the same way about you," she said boldly. "On both counts. You need to be safe too, Dex. Promise me that you won't put yourself in harm's way beyond what's necessary to achieve your objectives."

"You have my word." He grinned. "I have too much to live for to take any foolish risks," he insisted. "I'm looking at the best example of that that I know."

Katrina blushed. He seemed to always be able to charm his way out of any worry on her part. She supposed that played a big part in making her feel as she did about him. "Mahalo," she murmured. "I'll go to my suite and catch up on some chores till you tell me the danger has passed."

Dex nodded, satisfied. "Good."

Katrina walked away, glancing over her shoulder as he got on his cell phone and conferred with others on their plan of action. The entire thing made her nervous, quite frankly. She hoped it would be over quickly with no bloodshed at the lodge and the drug trafficker who fed Joseph's habit brought to justice.

DEX SAT CASUALLY at the Kahiko Lounge table alongside Lynda and Ishikawa, since their true identities had been revealed to Katrina. She had taken it well and intimated to Dex that it didn't come as a total shock, as she had suspected that he wasn't working alone in investigating drug trafficking at the lodge and on the island. *Good insight on her part*, Dex thought, resisting a smile, and feeling it was but one reason why he was so taken with her. The other reasons, such as personality, courage and vision, were just as important to him in the attraction. Not to mention being great in bed.

His thoughts returned to the present as he engaged in faux small talk with his colleagues, all pretending to be nursing cocktails, which were actually nonalcoholic tropical drinks. Other undercover law enforcement was in various degrees of pretending to be vacationers or staff throughout the Maoli Lodge. The hope was that this would all go peacefully. The suspect would pick up his cocaine dessert and exit with no fanfare and no one getting hurt. But Dex had been around long enough to know that the best laid plans could fall apart quickly. It was in that regard contingency tactics were in place to apprehend the suspect before he ever had a chance to grab his weapon, assuming he was armed. And Dex always assumed that where it concerned offenders in the drug trade.

Whatever went down, Dex's first priority was to see to it that not a hair on Katrina's precious head was harmed. Much less, the rest of her body. He was happy that she had cooperated with him without much fuss about staying put in her loft suite until this was over and her lodge was clear of the threat. While he knew the investigation was far from over, Dex needed to know for his own peace of mind that Katrina was safe and sound. He cared for her too much to wish for anything less. Quite the contrary, he was beginning to believe that there really could be light at the end of the tunnel when it came to getting the woman of his dreams and having a life that didn't revolve around battling drug dealers and the like. Maybe he had done enough, in memory of Rita, toward getting drugs off the streets and preventing some other young people from falling prey to addiction and dying. Maybe it was time he looked in a different direction in living life to the fullest. One that included Katrina.

But for now, he was still Special Agent Dex Adair and he had a job to do. At ten o'clock sharp, he watched as a tall and fit Hawaiian male entered the Kahiko Lounge. He had thick black hair in a messy hairstyle and a full goatee. The suspect wore a blue muscle tank T-shirt, athletic fit jeans and gray-black running sneakers.

"It's showtime," Dex said to the team as the suspect approached the bar's counter, where the cake sat.

"With a front row seat, all that's missing is the popcorn," Ishikawa quipped.

"Or ice cream to go with the cake," Lynda did him one better, before getting serious. "Let's get this done."

"We'll follow his lead," Dex said, "and go from there." He sent off a text to notify other law enforcement to stand down, but be on alert.

The suspect known only as Julio chatted in a friendly manner with Gordon briefly, who kept up his end of the bargain in not arousing suspicion. After the suspect looked around cautiously, he lifted the sheet cake and headed out of the lounge.

"He's on the move." Dex alerted Pietz on his cell phone. "Don't apprehend!" he emphasized.

"We'll let him go," the detective assured Dex, "see where he takes the cocaine."

Once the wheels were in motion, Dex, Lynda and Ishikawa left the table and followed the suspect without giving him a clue that they were on to him. Julio headed outside, where undercover agents did nothing to stop him from entering a black Jeep Grand Cherokee. It occurred to Dex that Katrina had believed that someone driving a vehicle of that color, make and model, had followed her that day. Could Julio have been her stalker? He didn't seem to fit with her description of the stalker as a white male, Dex considered. This led him to believe that the person who left Katrina the warning messages could have been working in tandem with Julio. If so, what did he get out of surveilling her? Could it have been a power play to undermine Julio or others in the drug organization?

Dex and the team rode together in his car in pursuit of the suspect, leading the way at a safe distance. All were armed and wearing bulletproof vests in preparation for a possible shoot-out. Dex kept in mind his promise to Katrina to not do anything foolish in the line of duty. He fully intended to honor that, but also knew that going after violent and seasoned drug offenders did not come without risk. This time was no different. Still, Dex was confident that with the heavily armed law enforcement in on the operation, his own chances for survival were pretty good.

"Where do you think he's taking his drug stash?" Lynda asked from the passenger seat.

"Could be anywhere," Dex responded honestly. "Most likely, it's somewhere nearby, where he can unload the cocaine quickly and distribute it accordingly."

"That's my way of thinking," Ishikawa agreed from the back seat, where he was keeping Barnabas company. "His cake is too hot to handle for very long."

"Not without getting burned," Dex said humorlessly. But just as he let out the words, he noted that the Jeep Grand Cherokee had suddenly picked up speed. The suspect was clearly attempting to flee. "Damn, we've been made." Dex made a face, wondering if he should have held back a bit more.

"So it seems," Lynda groaned, and then used her cell phone to notify the others in pursuit.

Dex pressed down on the accelerator to keep pace. "You can run, but you can't hide," he snapped.

"Not as long as he's on this island!" Ishikawa roared. "And I'm pretty sure the perp hasn't developed wings like a bird."

"If so, they've been clipped," Dex said. He found himself darting through traffic as the suspect drove at a high speed through the streets of Poipu as if he could somehow lose them. With an attempt by members of the police department to cut him off ahead,

Dex was more concerned about innocent people being hit by the drug trafficker's vehicle.

When it appeared as though they had him boxed in, the suspect somehow managed to elude capture and doubled back toward the Maoli Lodge. Dex's pulse raced as he imagined in his worst fears that Katrina might still be in danger should they fail to stop him. Then the suspect veered away from the lodge and sped off in another direction.

"Looks like the perp's headed for the storage unit I surveilled," Ishikawa called out. "Something told me there was more going on inside than keeping some old books and antiques in boxes."

"Could be you've hit the mark," Dex offered, preferring that to the lodge, as the lineup of official vehicles were in hot pursuit.

The fleeing suspect drove the Jeep into the parking lot of the storage facility on Koloa Road in Kalaheo, a quaint town not far from Poipu. With the cocaine coffee cake in hand, he darted inside the unit.

Dex parked away from the Jeep, fearing it could be booby-trapped. Exiting with Lynda and Ishikawa, they removed their weapons and used the car as cover, while waiting for the arrival of other law enforcement.

"Wonder who else is in there with him?" Ishikawa questioned.

"I'm betting he's not alone," Lynda warned.

Dex peered at the door of the facility. "And apparently has no intention of surrendering."

"That will be entirely up to him," Pietz declared bluntly from behind them. "We sure as hell won't wait around while he thinks about it. Not on my watch."

"I feel the same," Dex affirmed, not wanting to see the suspect find any way to climb out of the hole he'd dug for himself.

After coordinating with members of the Task Force on hand, the team, equipped with Glock pistols, Remington 870 shotguns, Smith & Wesson double-action semiautos, and Rock River Arms LAR-15 carbines, surrounded the facility. Without the element of surprise on their side and no desire to give anyone inside more of an opportunity to flush the evidence down the drain, Dex watched as Pietz nodded it was time to go in and do their business as officers of the law.

They used a battering ram to break open the door and entered the spacious storage unit in a flurry of actions, commands, chaos and exchange of gunfire with the two male individuals inside. They included the suspect in question and a stocky Asian man in his midthirties with short bleached blond hair worn in a Samurai bun. Both were armed with high-powered weapons and refused to surrender without a fight. They got just that. When it was over, both were mortally wounded before either could be interrogated about the drug-trafficking enterprise and other participants still at large. Not to mention, Dex had hoped to grill the suspect known only as Julio about both his assumed role in giving drugs to Joseph Sizemore and his possible connection to Katrina's stalker.

On the plus side, the dead suspects left behind a treasure trove of evidence of illegal activity that Dex figured might take a while to go through, but yield important information in the fight against drug trafficking. He brought in his K-9 pal to help sniff out more illicit drugs, which he did. Apart from finding the approximately four pounds of cocaine as a sheet cake, still largely intact, Barnabas helped them to locate yet more cocaine, along with a fair amount of hydrocodone, oxycodone, methamphetamine and fentanyl. The thought of the drugs making their way to users and turning them into addicts and criminals sickened Dex, thinking about his sister. He took solace in the fact that these illegal drugs would never harm a soul.

"Look what else they gave us," Lynda practically gushed, as she held in a nitrile-gloved hand a 9mm "ghost gun"—a self-assembled firearm without a commercial serial number.

Dex acknowledged the find. "I take it there's more of them?"

"You bet. Along with a cache of illegal weapons, I spotted a couple of Bushmaster .223 5.56mm-caliber AR-15 rifles and a HS Produkt .45-caliber handgun, among other firearms, along with rounds and magazines of ammo."

"There's also a boatload of cash as drug profits and for buying more weapons," Ishikawa said, walking up to the two.

"Quite a haul," Dex said, pleased. "Too bad they'll never get to use it."

Pietz joined them. "True, but this is just a drop in the bucket for these guys. Or those still amongst the living. They'll take the hit, lament over their losses and regroup. But not before we deal them more pain," he said intently. "We're still trying to track down the woman who delivered the bogus cake and any other associates."

"Once word spreads about what just went down, she's likely going to try to go underground," Lynda speculated.

Dex pursed his lips. "We can't allow that to happen," he insisted. "We need to beat the traffickers to the punch by disrupting their plans for escape and business as usual." In his way of thinking, that meant tracking down the ringleaders. Dex had a feeling that the two men killed were just foot soldiers, with someone else calling the shots. Until such person or persons were identified and apprehended, this case couldn't be put to rest. Nor would he feel Katrina was out of the woods, as long as the stalker was still out there, as if waiting for the right time and place to resurface.

Chapter Fourteen

Dex had texted Katrina to tell her that the coast was clear, insofar as her freedom of movement at the Maoli Lodge. Apparently, the suspect and a second person had been trapped and taken down at a storage facility. Thankfully, she had been spared the details. She relished being able to go about her business in the face of a tense situation between a suspected drug dealer and the authorities. But it still bothered her that this continued to hang over her and the lodge like a dark cumulus cloud. Dex had assured her that she had nothing to worry about and that they were on the verge of breaking the back of the drug cartel. But seeing was believing.

Until then, Katrina vowed to keep things as normal as possible as she entered the Kahiko Lounge. A few guests were seated with no drama to speak of. As she understood it, the operation inside the lounge went off without a hitch. Meaning few, if any, tourists were none the wiser in enjoying their stay and the amenities provided. Katrina greeted each of them as the owner and made her way to the bar, where Gordon was flirting with a pretty African American waitress named Rosalee DuBois, who was clearly eating up his words.

"Hey, Katrina." Rosalee flashed a big smile, with a brunette Afro blowout hairstyle shimmering.

"Aloha, Rosalee." She smiled back at her.

The slender waitress lifted a tray full of mai tais and walked away.

Katrina turned to Gordon, who asked with concern, "Are you okay?"

"Yes, I'm fine," she responded, glancing at the piano and picturing Dex sitting there and filling the lounge with sweet music. He really had been a good fit in that capacity. But there was no turning back, was there? In this case, she believed it was for the better, as Katrina had warmed up in a big way to the man as she saw him now.

"So, how long have you known Dex was an undercover DEA agent?" Gordon asked, as if reading her thoughts.

Katrina faced the bartender. "Long enough," she admitted. "I was sworn to secrecy while he did his job."

"Figured as much."

She tucked some strands of hair behind an ear. "Mahalo for going along with the operation. I'm sure it helped keep things from getting out of hand."

Gordon shrugged. "Did what I needed to." He used a cloth towel to wipe off the counter. "If I'd suspected the cake was cocaine, I never would have allowed her to leave it."

"I know." Katrina offered him a grateful smile. "Guess we all need to be more on guard against these types of things in the future." How desperate were drug dealers that they needed to be so creative in order to hide and distribute their product?

"You're right. My bad." He eyed her sorrowfully. "In any event, I heard they nailed the dude."

"I heard that too." She gulped, wishing it hadn't come down to a violent confrontation. "Maybe something good can come out of this if more and more people can educate themselves about the horrors of drug use and addiction." She couldn't help but think about Dex's sister. Having her die that way and not being able to do anything about it must have been devastating. Just as it was for her to discover that Joseph had been using drugs, which may have led to his falling out of the kayak and drowning.

"Yeah, I'm with you there," Gordon told her. "Better get back to it."

"You and me both," Katrina said, waving goodbye and greeting other guests as she left the lounge. She played host in the lobby before heading back to her office.

When she felt a hand on her shoulder before entering the office, she jumped and turned to see Alyson standing there with a frown on her face. "Mind telling me what just happened at the lodge?"

Katrina batted her eyes innocently. "Excuse me?"

"There was some commotion," she voiced. "One of the guests said that the authorities raided the place—is that true?"

"No. Not exactly."

Alyson looked nonplussed. "What does that mean?"

Katrina ushered her into the office so they could speak in private. She decided there was no reason to withhold what others already knew or apparently figured out, in spite of the surreptitious nature of the stakeout. "Someone left cocaine disguised as a sheet cake at the lodge," she told her. "When a man came to pick it up, the feds and members of the Kauai PD watched and allowed him to leave, but followed. Apparently, there was a wild car chase and things came to a head at a storage facility, where the suspect and another drug trafficker were holed up. It ended there with them being killed..." She shuddered at the thought that Dex could have lost his own life in the gun battle, but had managed to come away unharmed, thankfully.

"You should have given me a heads-up on this operation," Alyson griped. "It would have been nice to have had some sort of advance warning so I wouldn't have freaked out wondering what was going on."

"It wasn't my place to spill the beans prematurely, without jeopardizing the mission," Katrina countered, though sympathetic to her assistant manager's point of view. "I'm sorry you were left out of the loop."

Alyson sighed. "I'm the one who should be apologizing," she insisted abruptly. "Didn't mean to overstep. You had every right to follow the lead of the authorities in this matter."

"No harm." Katrina offered her a friendly smile. "We've all been a bit on edge of late. Hopefully, we can turn the page now and get back to the business of running a lodge without the threat of drug trafficking in our midst." At least that was the plan, as far as she was concerned. But in the back of her mind, Katrina feared that this wasn't over yet, in spite of her wishes to the contrary.

"I can't argue with you there," Alyson agreed. "Anything of that sort is obviously bad for business. I'm glad the police put a stop to it before the situation could get any worse."

"That, they did." Katrina couldn't help but wonder if whatever secrets Julio held regarding Joseph's final hours would now be buried forever, along with the two men.

They went to their respective desks and Alyson quickly moved on to discussing upcoming work on the landscaping.

"WE RAN THEIR PRINTS," Lynda told Dex a couple of hours later regarding the two men killed at the storage facility shootout. "And, not too surprisingly, considering their chosen profession, we got a hit."

"I'm listening," Dex said anxiously, as they conferred at the Kauai PD headquarters to get some details on the criminal suspects.

She glanced at a laptop on the table. "The Asian male is identified as Freddie Bautista. Age thirty-six and Filipino American. Using the FBI's Advanced Fingerprint Identification Technology, we learned that Bautista has priors in Hawaii and New York for drug-related offenses, such as possession with the intent to distribute meth and selling counterfeit oxycodone pills containing fentanyl."

"Sounds like a real piece of work." Dex's forehead creased, looking at his mug shot. "What about the one who took off with the cocaine cake?" he asked interestedly.

"Full name's Eduardo Julio Nihei," she said, putting his info on the screen. "Age thirty-two. Has a long rap sheet with everything from drug-related to weapons-related offenses. Nihei was wanted in Arizona on distribution of fentanyl and possessing ecstasy and meth for distribution."

Dex had used his cell phone to take a picture of the dead perp, with the information virtually cinching the connection between Nihei and Joseph Sizemore. So, Julio spoon-fed Sizemore the meth and fentanyl? Was the intent to commit murder? Or to keep the late lodge co-owner hooked and unable to know what was possibly happening all around him in plain view? "They say the dead can't speak, but Nihei seems to be saying plenty from the morgue," Dex commented tongue in cheek, "about his role as a trafficker of drugs in Poipu, Kalaheo and elsewhere on the island."

"He and Bautista definitely weren't acting alone," Lynda informed him. "I've done a little digging and see that Nihei has an older brother named Rafael Carlos Nihei. He, too, has a history of drug-involved criminality, violence and racketeering." She put his mug shot on the screen and Dex saw that he resembled Julio, only his face was fuller and he had a French crop haircut and was clean-shaven. "The elder Nihei is thought to be trafficking drugs between the Hawaiian Islands and the mainland, while operating out of Kauai."

"Which means Julio was working for his brother," Dex stated, "and not the other way around."

"That's the way I'm reading it," she said.

Dex was thoughtful. "And the same is likely true for the unsub who's been stalking Katrina. He obviously has more insight into me and our operation than I'm comfortable with."

Lynda nodded. "Whoever he is, the walls are beginning to close in on the entire drug-trafficking operation. And he'll be another casualty, one way or another."

"We'll see about that," Dex muttered, still having an uneasy feeling in that regard while Katrina's safety was on the line.

Ishikawa entered the room, his eyes shifting back and forth. "Just spoke with forensics about the Jeep Grand Cherokee Eduardo Nihei was driving. So far, the only legible prints they've come up with belonged to Nihei and Freddie Bautista."

Dex frowned. "I was afraid you'd say that." He was sure it was the same vehicle as the one driven by Katrina's stalker. "What about DNA?"

"They're still looking into that."

Dex sighed. "What about the cake delivery woman?"

Ishikawa plopped into a chair. "According to Clayton Pietz, they should have a name and location anytime now."

"Good." Dex hoped to interrogate her sooner than later to see what light she could shed on the organization and its participants. At the same time, he feared that the unsub was expendable, as Rafael Nihei started to feel the heat with the death of his brother. Along with the screws tightening at every turn of his crumbling world of illicit drug distribution.

WHILE IN LIHUE, Dex popped over to Larry's Aquatic Shop, where he tracked down Larry Nakanishi, who was stocking a shelf. No longer needing to remain undercover, Dex flashed his identification and said, pulling no punches, "DEA Special Agent Dex Adair."

"Why am I not surprised?" Larry flinched. "Are you here to arrest me for using meth at one time?"

Dex gave a humorless chuckle. "Lucky you, I'm not interested in your previous or even current drug use, if you had a relapse," he told him truthfully.

Larry exhaled. "Well, if you're still investigating Joseph's death, I've already told you everything I know."

"Maybe not everything." Dex took out his cell phone and pulled up the picture he'd taken of Eduardo Julio Nihei's mug shot. "Is this Julio, the man you say sold Joseph Sizemore the meth the day he died after the kayaking accident?" Dex waited a beat. "Take a good look."

Apparently, Larry needed no time to ponder, as he responded with certitude the moment he saw the mug shot. "Yeah, that's definitely Julio." Dex figured as much, but needed to hear it from the person who was with Sizemore that fateful day. Larry looked at him. "Is he back on the island?"

"Maybe he never left," Dex suggested, scrutinizing him. "Why? You thinking about hooking up with him again for some meth?"

Larry scowled. "No way. I'm done with the stuff," he maintained. "Just wondering, that's all."

"Julio's dead," Dex almost hated to inform him. On second thought, lessons learned, he hoped. "His days of dealing drugs are over." He watched Larry lean awkwardly on one foot in perturbed silence, before Dex said, "I'll let you get back to stocking shelves." He left the shop on that note, armed with further information in making a solid connection between Nihei and Katrina's late husband as part of the broader picture of trafficking drugs on the island.

BACK AT THE LODGE, Dex acknowledged Lynda and Ishikawa, who, in spite of their identities as DEA agents being revealed to Katrina, continued to keep up their facade as married tourists while maintaining a watchful eye for any signs of trouble that might have arisen after the takedown of Eduardo Julio Nihei. By all appearances, things looked peaceful as Dex walked around with Barnabas on a leash. Yet there was an uneasy feeling in the pit of his stomach that Nihei's brother, or perhaps the stalker, might try to retaliate for the two drug dealers' deaths or the financial losses incurred from the drug bust.

Not spotting her, Dex sent Katrina a text asking if they could talk in her suite. She replied yes and said she would meet him there in five minutes. He waited by her door with Barnabas as fresh memories ran through Dex's head of the blazing intimacy between him and Katrina. She was special and he would do everything in his power to keep her alive and well. That started with keeping her abreast of where things stood in the investigation.

"Hey," Dex heard the tender sound of Katrina's voice.

"Hey." He grinned as she approached. "Hope you weren't too busy?"

"Not too busy." Katrina's eyes twinkled. "Some things are more important than others."

"I agree." In his book, she was one of those things. Dex was starting to realize that more and more with each passing day.

Inside, he commanded Barnabas to sit and, as always, the dog was obedient and eager to please. They sat side by side on the sectional, where Dex recalled first coming clean about being a DEA agent and investigating drug trafficking and the death of Roxanne. The fact that Katrina had initially been a suspect was something Dex wished he could take back, given what he knew now. But she had apparently never held that against him, for which he was beyond appreciative. He wanted to be a part of her life now and maybe much more.

"I'm glad you're here in one piece after your confrontation," she said, soft worry lines creasing her forehead.

"So am I." He chewed on his lower lip. "As for the way things went down, if there had been any other way, I would've preferred to take them in alive."

"I believe you." Katrina put her hand on the knee of his linen pants. "You have to do your job. No one could fault that."

Dex nodded to that effect and said evenly, "The dead drug dealer who picked up the cake is the same one who supplied Joseph with meth and fentanyl. His full name is Eduardo Julio Nihei. Larry Nakanishi confirmed his identity." Dex removed the cell phone from his back pocket and showed her Nihei's mug shot. "Have you seen him before?"

"I don't think so." Katrina shook her head, grimacing. "I just can't believe Joseph got mixed up with the likes of him."

"I know." Dex sympathized with her. "When it comes to drug use and addiction, many have a tendency to get involved with the wrong people." His sister came to mind, as was often the case.

"Yeah, I guess," she groaned, contemplative.

He showed her the mug shots of Julio's brother, Rafael Carlos Nihei, and Freddie Bautista, identifying the latter as the other fatality in the storage unit. "Have you seen either of these men before?"

Katrina sat back. "Neither rings a bell," she indicated and gazed at Dex. "Should I have?"

"Not really." He rubbed his jawline. "I wondered if the man who's been stalking you could have been one or the other?" Dex asked doubtfully.

Her lashes danced above wide eyes. "Uh, not unless he's a chameleon with his complexion. Other than that, the person who was stalking me is someone else."

"I suspected as much." Dex didn't mean to question her judgment. "Had to be sure," he stressed, as they continued to try and connect the mystery man to the drug-trafficking probe.

"I understand," she said, her features brightening. "I haven't gotten any more notes or been shadowed by him. Could be that whatever his intentions, he's turned his attention elsewhere."

"I'd like to believe that," Dex told her, stretching an arm across the top of the sofa.

"But you don't…?" Her voice cracked with unease. She could read him well, so he wasn't going to downplay the threat the man still posed to her safety. "Let's just say that until the unsub is eliminated as a person of interest and you no longer have to look over your shoulder at every turn, I'll keep him in the crosshairs."

Katrina beamed and ran a hand along the side of his face. "Mahalo."

"Just keeping it real," Dex claimed, knowing it went much further than that. She had become someone he couldn't get out of his mind. And didn't want to. Whatever their future, he was bound to protecting her in the present.

"Yes, let's keep it real, Dex." She inched closer to him, tilted his chin and planted a firm kiss on his mouth before pulling back. "Is that real enough for you?"

He grinned, tasting the sweetness of the kiss. "Yeah, about as real as it gets. In fact, maybe we need to try that again."

"Good idea," Katrina murmured, and leaned into him, whereby this time Dex was more than happy to take the lead. With a hand behind her neck, he brought them together and their mouths opened onto each other's for a searing kiss that turned his heart and soul upside down. If he hadn't known it before, he did now. He had fallen in love with her and would need to process it in relation to the cards on the table, that defined their lives at this time.

Just as his introspection gave way to the passions and sounds of their lips locked, Dex's cell phone buzzed. He wanted to simply ignore it, hoping it might go away, but given the serious nature of his current assignment, that wasn't an option. Taking his mouth off Katrina's, Dex said apologetically, "I need to get that."

She touched her slightly open lips dazedly. "Please do."

He grabbed the phone off the sectional and saw that the caller was Detective Pietz. "Hey," Dex said coolly, standing and turning his back toward Katrina.

"We've got a bead on the woman who delivered the cocaine sheet cake," Pietz informed him. "Laurie Hoapili. Age twenty-seven. She runs a bakery called Laurie's Baked Treats in Hanapepe. We believe she was working for Rafael Carlos Nihei, along with his brother, Eduardo. I'm sending you a photo of her now..." Dex received it and studied the face. A pretty woman, she had bold brown eyes and long raven hair in a beach waves style. "We're headed to the bakery now with a warrant for Ms. Hoapili's arrest and a narcotics-related felony search warrant, if you and your team want in on this."

"We'll meet you there," Dex told him.

"And bring along your K-9 buddy, Barnabas," the detective said. "We may need him."

"Will do. See you soon." Dex disconnected and turned to Katrina, reading the curious expression on her face.

"What was that all about?" she asked, getting to her feet.

"The police have identified the woman who delivered the cocaine cake to the lodge this morning." He showed her the photograph on his cell phone. "Name's Laurie Hoapili. I don't suppose you've seen her before?"

Katrina peered at the image and said forlornly, "I'm afraid not. Looks like I'm striking out in placing faces…"

"Actually, that's a good thing," Dex countered. "Means that none of these people have been regulars at the Maoli Lodge, disassociating it primarily with illicit drug activity."

"Yes, that is good to know," she said. "I'd never want the lodge to be thought of as some sort of drug haven for traffickers. Even if it was beyond my knowledge."

"Didn't think so." He smiled thinly. "Anyway, a raid is about to go down at the delivery woman's bakery. I need to be there."

She nodded, touching his chest. "Be careful."

"I will." Dex took her hand off him and kissed the back of it. He called Barnabas and the dog ran over to them. "We'll be back soon," he promised, even while wondering how long it would be and where they could take their relationship.

Without saying a word, Katrina gave him a going away present with a big kiss on the mouth, making sure Dex wouldn't go very far without thinking of being with her in every way possible.

Chapter Fifteen

Dex arrived at Laurie's Baked Treats on Hanapepe Road, accompanied by Lynda and Ishikawa. The area was swarming with members of armed law enforcement, which had evacuated nearby shops and residences out of an abundance of caution. With a heightened sense of urgency and uneasiness all around, following the gunfight that took place at the storage facility earlier, no one was taking any chances on innocent lives being lost. Or, for that matter, the safety of those tasked with serving the warrants and ending this peacefully.

Barnabas was kept in the car until proven safe for him to go into action, as Dex joined Pietz and others wearing bulletproof vests and carrying firearms in approaching the bakery. Though there was no outward indication that whoever was inside would rather fight to the death than give up, Dex wasn't sure which way this would go. All he knew for certain was that Katrina had given him a new reason for wanting to come out ahead in any potentially dan-

gerous mission. Yes, he wanted to rid the world—
or at least the United States—of the scourge of drug
abuse and trafficking. But one person could only do
so much. He wanted more to make his life worth-
while. With Katrina, Dex believed he just might have
that more than he could have ever imagined.

"Listen up," Pietz said. "A delivery truck and a
white Dodge Charger, both registered to the suspect, are parked in the back, suggesting she's inside
the building."

Dex thought about seeing the delivery truck at the
lodge before realizing just what the woman was up
to. If he could do it over again, maybe he could have
caught her prior to reaching this point. "She might
not be alone," he said, with the possibility that other
unsubs or employees and customers could be inside.
Any of whom could be used as hostages or shields.

"We've got a hostage negotiator ready and able to
step in if needed," Pietz told him. "So far, there's no
indication there are any customers inside."

"That's good," Dex said, not wanting to risk a
bloodbath.

"Which is why we need to be quick and decisive,"
the detective warned. "Can't allow her to try and hide
behind others. Or slip through our grasp."

"Don't see the latter happening," Ishikawa insisted, holding his weapon toward the ground. "She's
someone who may be able to lead us to Rafael Carlos Nihei."

"That's the plan. Okay," Pietz told those leading the brigade, "let's do this."

Dex was onboard, bracing himself as they approached the bakery's front door. It was locked. Even in the apparent absence of customers, the whereabouts of the suspect was still in question, giving him reason to be concerned.

The door was forced open with a Halligan bar before Dex and Pietz rushed inside, their firearms ready to use, if necessary. The bakery was dimly lit with guava malasadas, cookies, doughnuts, cream puffs and other tasty treats on display. But no sign of the owner. They believed she might be hiding in the kitchen. Or in the company of other drug traffickers, perhaps waiting to ambush them.

When Pietz nodded at him, Dex shouted ahead as they approached cautiously, "Laurie Hoapili, this is DEA Special Agent Adair. We have a warrant for your arrest. Come out with your hands up and this can end without anyone getting hurt."

There was no response. And no indication that she wasn't alone. It seemed reasonable to Dex that the suspect may have already fled on foot or in a different vehicle, anticipating the raid. Or been tipped off by someone, perhaps from the inside. The idea that one of their own could have been in cahoots with the drug cartel bothered Dex. But he couldn't dismiss the possibility altogether, in spite of hoping otherwise.

They burst into the kitchen and there was no gunfire aimed at them. A quick scan showed Dex just the usual trappings of a bakery, with its baked goods and equipment. It was only as he made his way around a rectangle stainless steel table, that he spotted the body sprawled on the floor. The slender female's head was lying in a pool of blood. Beside it was a handgun that looked to be a Luger 9mm pistol. Turning back to the unmoving victim, he recognized her as the woman suspected of delivering the cocaine coffee sheet cake to the Maoli Lodge. Laurie Hoapili.

To Dex, it appeared to be a suicide, but he was taking nothing for granted. Once the bakery was deemed clear of any other victims or possible assailants, and potential evidence of the killing preserved, he employed his K-9 cop to search for any drugs on the premises. As expected, the canine delivered in discovering hidden in the refrigerator and a back storage room, countless vape cartridges containing more than 80 percent tetrahydrocannabinol or THC, as labeled, many grams of psilocybin mushrooms, pounds of marijuana and fentanyl, and medicated edibles.

"Looks like this place was offering a lot more than glazed doughnuts and guava malasadas," Pietz said humorously.

"Yeah, mix and match, according to your tastes," Dex said dryly, holding Barnabas on a leash.

"A perfect front for manufacturing, collecting and distributing illicit drugs," Lynda reasoned.

"Tell me about it," Ishikawa tsked. "Then they pass it out like candy across the island, the other

Hawaiian Islands and the mainland, getting filthy rich in the process."

Dex grimaced, while weighing the items confiscated, including nearly a dozen firearms, such as semiautomatic rifles and other weapons. "I think the traffickers' luck is just about ready to run its course." At least this was his fervent wish. But he knew there were still more hoops to climb through before any of them could take a bow.

Twenty minutes later, Dex's fears on the cause of death were confirmed by the medical examiner, Francesca Espanto, who examined the victim at the scene. "Once the autopsy has been completed, I'll be able to give you my final report, but in my preliminary exam of the decedent, based on the angle and size of the wound to the side of the head and proximity of the firearm on the floor, I'd say in all likelihood Ms. Hoapili's fatal injuries were self-inflicted by a gunshot."

"I'd already come to that conclusion," he told her sadly, preferring that they would have had a chance to interrogate the bakery owner.

"Hoapili obviously felt the pressure of the drug-trafficking operation about to blow up in their faces," Pietz surmised, "and decided to check out before she could be arrested and sent to prison."

Dex did not disagree, but added, "With another box checked in dismantling the drug-trafficking ring on Kauai, we still need to track down the ringleader, Rafael Carlos Nihei. As well as his associates…"

"We will." The detective sounded confident. "We've just turned up the heat a few notches. Something tells me that Nihei knows we're coming for him and is looking for a way out—but won't find it."

"I'll second that." Dex wanted to see the drug trafficker, who undoubtedly ordered the hit on Roxanne Yamamoto and caused Katrina more stress and strain than she deserved, brought to his knees. Along with any others in his orbit, such as Katrina's stalker, who may have been vying for control of the organization and saw her as a convenient means to an end as the proprietor of the Maoli Lodge while under investigation. As such, Dex felt the man was still unpredictable, in spite of no further attempts to contact or surveil her of late. That made him dangerous. Possibly to Katrina, giving Dex cause for concern.

KATRINA WAS STILL trying to come to terms with Joseph's involvement with drug dealer Eduardo Julio Nihei, who may or may not have been introduced to him by Larry Nakanishi. Just how long had Joseph been using? And would he have ever sought help had he lived? Then there were some of the other players in the drug business, Julio's brother, Rafael Carlos Nihei, and Freddie Bautista. Not to mention Laurie Hoapili, the woman who brought a sheet cake of cocaine to the lodge. Katrina hoped that once she had been arrested, she might be able to shed more light on the ins and outs of the business. Or was there a code of silence among drug dealers?

As Katrina resumed her duties as host to new arrivals, her head was spinning as she thought about
the life she once had with Joseph that was left behind with his death. *I just need to forgive him and
move on,* she told herself, feeling there was no other
choice. It was time for her to focus more on what she
wanted for the rest of her life. Quite simply, it was
to find love and be loved by someone who wouldn't
betray her trust when the chips were down. Maybe
someone to start a family with. Was that asking too
much? Or not enough? Did Dex have what it took
to make her feelings for him stand the test of time?

While pondering those conflicting thoughts, she
headed across the lobby, surprised when her cell
phone chimed. She reached for it in the pocket of
her one-button charcoal blazer. She saw that Dex
was requesting a video chat and quickly accepted it,
eager to know that he and his K-9 companion were
all right and they had located the delivery woman.
"Hey," she said, gazing at his handsome face filling
the small screen as she moved away from others toward a collection of areca palms.

"Hey. Wanted to let you know we were able to
find Laurie Hoapili." His features darkened. "I'm
afraid she's dead. The medical examiner believes it
was suicide. I have no reason to dispute that."

"Oh dear." Katrina's heart lurched as she pondered the finality of it. Taking one's own life was
never the answer, no matter what issues they faced.

"I wish she'd given herself a chance to turn her life around."

"So do I. Unfortunately, casualties are par for the course in the illegal drug trade," Dex asserted.

"I guess," she said, still troubled by it coming so soon after Roxanne's death.

"She left behind more evidence that we hope will lead to arrests and putting the drug traffickers out of commission on and around Kauai."

"Yes, that would be a blessing." Katrina took a breath as she wondered what would become of them when that happened. Had he thought about it in a serious way? Or should she just let it play out…whatever was meant to be?

"Well, I have to go," Dex told her, and abruptly turned the cell phone to show Barnabas. "Like me, he can't wait to spend more time with you."

She smiled. "I feel the same way about both of you."

"Cool." Dex favored her with a boyish grin. "What do you like on your pizza?"

"Hmm…" She thought about it, in spite of not being a big pizza lover. "How about fresh basil and black olives?"

"Sure, I can work with that." He laughed. "Along with maybe some sausage and extra cheese."

"Sounds good," she told him.

"Same here. See you soon."

After they disconnected, Katrina smiled, relishing another opportunity to have a meal with him. She wondered naughtily what they might want to do for dessert. And even beyond, she considered, because it appeared as though the investigation into drug trafficking was nearing its conclusion. Their future was something they would definitely need to talk about.

Her cell phone chimed while she was still holding it, indicating she had a text message. Her pulse raced as she read it,

This isn't over. Don't let down your guard. Still a target, like your late husband. Be smart. Adair can't always protect. No one can. I'm watching you.

Nearly dropping the phone out of trepidation, Katrina's knees buckled as she looked around, expecting to find the man who was stalking her and apparently threatening again with this text after the earlier messages. She saw no sign of him. At least not one that was recognizable. Could he be wearing a disguise? She examined faces of those milling about or passing through. Could be any one of the younger and fit men, she supposed. *Am I a sitting duck right now?* Katrina asked herself with dread, as she moved quickly away from the lobby.

She nearly ran smack-dab into Alyson, who asked perceptively, "What is it?"

Katrina was tongue-tied with anxiety. "The stalker just sent me a text," she stammered, and showed it to her.

"Seriously?" Alyson's lips pursed with anger.

"I think he's inside the lodge," Katrina said, shuddering.

The assistant manager scanned the area. "I don't see anyone acting suspicious. Maybe this creep is just toying with you for who knows what sick reason."

Though she almost found that preferable, Katrina sensed that he was trying to tell her something. But what exactly? That Joseph had, in fact, been a murder victim? And that someone was trying to kill her too? If so, why? Was she powerless to protect herself, even with Dex in her corner and seemingly on the verge of bringing down the drug cartel? Or was this even about that?

"I'm going to my room," she told Alyson anxiously, believing she would be safe there until Dex returned. "Can you handle things for now?"

Alyson frowned. "Yes, but—"

"Mahalo," Katrina said, cutting her off, feeling very vulnerable at the moment and wanting only to keep an apparent enemy at a somewhat safe distance.

"WE'VE GOT AN interesting hit on DNA pulled off the dashboard of the Jeep Grand Cherokee that Eduardo Julio Nihei was driving," Lynda informed Dex from the passenger side of his vehicle.

"Go on…" He glanced away from the road and at her as she studied a laptop. Ishikawa had volunteered to dog-sit Barnabas, who needed some fresh air.

"It belongs to Zachary Lawrence, according to

the FBI's CODIS DNA database and DNA Case-work Unit."

"Why does that name ring a bell?" Dex asked, searching his memory.

"Because he's one of us," she pointed out. "At least he used to be. Two years ago, the then forty-year-old Lawrence was a DEA special agent with the Phoenix division. After his wife and daughter were killed during a botched robbery, he went rogue. Was initially suspended for allegedly pocketing drug money from raids on drug traffickers. Though no charges were ever filed, he was fired and basically went off the map. Till now."

"Hmm…" Dex was thoughtful. He had never met the man but was familiar with the case. Being a dirty DEA agent was debatably even worse than the stan-dard scumbags who trafficked in drugs for profit. Had Lawrence really fallen this low as a bitter and greedy ex agent? "Can you pull up his picture?"

"Got it right here." Lynda turned the laptop around and Dex took a quick look at the image of Zachary Lawrence. His face was diamond-shaped and he had blue eyes and thick black hair in a slicked back style with a taper fade. "You think he's the mys-tery man who's been stalking Katrina and sending her messages?"

"Seems to fit her general description of him," Dex said, crossing an intersection on Ala Kalanikaumaka Street, "and someone who was in a position to know

I was a DEA agent he could expose and cause other trouble for Katrina. Only one way to know for sure."

"What would be his motivation?" Lynda wondered verbally. "Let me guess, to seize the perfect opportunity to cause confusion during our investigation, sowing seeds of doubt here and there—including the cause of Sizemore's death?"

"Maybe. Or because he has relevant information to share, but not at the expense of—or in spite of—his greater goal to be in control of the highly profitable drug operation by eliminating the competition." Dex mulled over the possibilities as he pulled into the pizza restaurant lot. "Whatever the case, something tells me that wherever Nihei is holed up, Lawrence is probably by his side and plotting to undermine him."

When his cell phone hummed as they stepped out of the car, Dex grabbed it and saw that it was Katrina. "Are you okay?" he asked, sensing otherwise.

"Just got a chilling text message from the stalker." Her voice shook. "I think he may be at the lodge."

"Where are you now?" Dex wondered if Lawrence would be so bold as to make a move in plain view.

"In my suite," Katrina responded.

"Stay put," he ordered. "I'm on my way."

"Was that Katrina?" Lynda gazed at him.

He nodded. "Someone, presumably Zachary Lawrence, just sent her a text. We better get back there now."

"Let's go," Lynda agreed gamely.

The pizza would have to wait, Dex felt, not willing to take any chances that Lawrence might try to harm Katrina if the opening was there, along with intent.

Chapter Sixteen

Once Katrina confirmed it was Dex on the other side of the door, she opened it and wrapped her arms around him, as if needing the reassurance of their bodies close together. "Thanks for coming," she uttered.

"Couldn't keep me away," he insisted, pulling them apart and going inside the suite.

"Where's the pizza?" Katrina asked, noting he was empty-handed and feeling guilty about that.

"We can have it delivered." Dex gave her a serious look. "Can I see the text message?"

"Have it right here." She had kept the cell phone on in her pocket, and removed it to show him.

Dex took the cell phone and read the words silently.

"They probably used a burner phone." Dex's brow furrowed, handing the phone back to her. "You never saw him?"

"Not to my knowledge." Her lips pursed. "He

could have been hiding, but still able to watch me." She sighed. "What do you make of this?"

His chin tautened. "I think I know who's behind it."

"Really?" She looked up at him tensely. "Who?"

He took out his own cell phone and showed her a photo. "Does this look like the man who followed you?"

Katrina studied the image and flashed back to that day at the shopping center when she was trying to get away from him. "Yes, I'm pretty sure that's him." She met Dex's eyes. "Who is he?"

"His name is Zachary Lawrence. He's a former DEA agent."

Shock registered across her face. "What?"

"Lawrence's DNA was found in the Jeep Grand Cherokee that Julio was driving," Dex informed her. "We believe it was likely the same Jeep that was following you."

Katrina tried to wrap her head around this. Why would an ex-DEA agent be sending her text messages and stalking her? "Do you know why he's chosen me to obsess on?" she queried.

Dex drew a breath. "Apparently, Lawrence jumped ship from good to bad following the deaths of his wife and daughter. And ended up stealing illicit drug money and evidently graduated into hardcore drug trafficking. How he got involved with the Nihei brothers and their operation on Kauai is anyone's guess."

She frowned. "I'm still not sure what any of that has to do with me? He says I'm a target and intimated that Joseph was too. What does any of this mean?"

Dex held her shoulders. "It means that we've now identified Zachary Lawrence, taking away his one and only advantage in terrorizing you. Until we find him, I won't let anything happen to you."

"Promise?" She gazed into his eyes, unblinking. Even then, Katrina understood that if this man was determined to get to her, Dex couldn't guarantee that it wouldn't happen. But hearing the words from him to that effect still gave her comfort.

"Count on it," he reaffirmed in a convincing tone.

Right now, what she needed most from him was the feel of his lips upon hers. This prompted Katrina to raise her chin so he could read her mind. Before she could give him a hint, Dex pulled her close and laid a ravenous kiss on her mouth, which she received wholeheartedly. If nothing else, it took them away from more pressing concerns for some intimate time. To Katrina, this was a welcome interlude and, she hoped, a harbinger for things to come in their lives together. They went to bed and made love with the same sense of urgency and sexual chemistry as before—only this time it was with even more energy and compatibility in satisfying their needs.

Instead of ordering pizza afterward, they slept and had leftovers, before more sex and sleeping through the night. Katrina was certain that, at some point, the word *love* passed through Dex's lips. Or was it her own in speaking from the heart? When morning came, neither broached the subject, and she wondered if it was all in her imagination. Or were they both merely waiting for the right time to delve into those feelings and what they meant in moving forward?

They were enjoying a hearty breakfast she'd made of taro pancakes, bacon and Ulu Fiti breadfruit, with coffee, when Dex asked casually, "Just to be on the safe side, would it be okay if I put a GPS tracker on your cell phone? Probably won't need to access it, but until we can fully neutralize the threat to your safety, I'd feel a lot better knowing where you are when we're apart."

Holding her mug, Katrina eyed him. "I'm fine with that." She welcomed giving him the ability to track her whereabouts right now. Especially with an ex-DEA agent seemingly unwilling to leave her alone. And his behavior could escalate to something more dangerous.

"Good." Dex grinned and grabbed a piece of bacon from the plate. "If it were up to me, I wouldn't let you out of my sight."

"And I wouldn't let you out of mine," Katrina teased, but meant every single word. Waking up to his good-looking face and getting to enjoy him all day long, every day, was something she relished the fantasy of as a reality.

"Nice to hear." He showed his teeth. "Be that as it

may, with duty calling, I've asked Lynda to shadow you today, if that's all right."

"Yes," she agreed, having felt comfortable around the DEA agent when chatting with her as a vacationer, even if Katrina preferred his company to anyone else's.

"After that, we'll see..."

She wondered if he was weighing where things stood between them and if sleeping in the same bed could turn into a more permanent arrangement. "You can stay here for the remainder of your time on the island, Dex," she volunteered, in case he had any doubt of her comfort level with him. "So can Barnabas."

"I appreciate the offer." He dug his fork into some taro pancakes musingly. "I'll let you know."

At least he's considering it, Katrina told herself, lifting the breadfruit, while wondering just how long this remarkable ride with an amazing man would last once his assignment was over.

Dex waited for Lynda to show up before leaving Katrina's loft suite. He really did wish he never had to leave her side, which was indicative of the strong feelings he was developing for the lodge owner. It wasn't lost on him that the *L*-word slipped from his mouth—and maybe hers too—during the night. This gave him hope that they were working toward something he never wanted to let go of. But right now, he needed to finish up the investigation and keep her safe, not necessarily in that order.

After picking up Barnabas from his overnight stay in Lynda and Ishikawa's room, Dex headed back to the cottage, where Ishikawa would join him later to compare notes. Once there, the cranky canine was let loose in the yard, after being sedentary too long inside. Dex looked around, not missing the place a bit since spending the past two nights at Katrina's. Before leaving the other day, he had put things back in order somewhat. Presumably, it had been ransacked by someone intending to send him a message. Was it Zachary Lawrence? Rafael Carlos Nihei? Or both, as partners in drug trafficking?

Whatever the case, Dex was not intimidated in the least. It was what he'd signed up for with the DEA. Still, it was all beginning to wear just a bit thin. He wanted more than this out of life. He had decided to take Katrina up on her offer to house him and Barnabas for the rest of their visit to Kauai, if for no other reason than to be able to stay close to her and ward off any threats to her life and security. Of course, there were other important reasons too for wanting to be in her presence. Not the least of which was that she made him happy, and feel as if there was a greater purpose to his life and a real ability and opportunity to share it with someone he considered an equal in all the ways that counted.

As Dex tossed his clothes into a leather duffel bag, he heard Barnabas barking. *What's he up to?* Dex wondered. Maybe chasing a gecko? Or perhaps a feral chicken, with thousands of them roaming around the island like they owned the place. He stopped packing and went into the backyard. The K-9 was jumping at a low hanging branch of a fig tree that managed to stay just out of his reach. Walking over to the dog, Dex checked out what was so captivating to him. There appeared to be something tied to the branch. What was that? He realized it was a small cotton pouch with a drawstring.

Using his height and long arm, Dex had no trouble reaching and grabbing it. Opening the pouch, while keeping it away from Barnabas, he sniffed and smelled the distinctive pungent odor of marijuana, but only saw a flash drive. What was it doing up in the tree? Had it been hidden there with important information by Roxanne as insurance should she run into trouble? How could he have missed that before?

Back inside, Dex sat down on a tufted leather wingback chair with his laptop and put in the flash drive. He saw two files. One was labeled "Special Agent Zachary Lawrence." His interest piqued, Dex opened it and watched anxiously as a video of the disgraced DEA agent materialized.

Lawrence, who sported a three-day stubble beard, was calm and collected as he said, "If you're watching this, Adair, it means your K-9 pooch did his drug-detection job and you're finally starting to figure things out. What took you so long? Or maybe you need a little help, which I'm here to provide. I'm DEA Special Agent Zachary Lawrence. I'm sure you've done your homework and drawn the wrong conclusions. No, I'm not a dirty agent. Just the opposite. I've been deep undercover for more than a year now, bouncing from one assignment to another, infiltrating illegal drug-trafficking operations and helping to bring the perps to justice. Your boss, Rachel Zavatti, whom I've been reporting to as well for the last six months, will vouch for me.

"Anyway, to make a long story short, yes, I'm the one who's been leaving Katrina Sizemore the cryptic notes and following her—not as some psycho stalker, but to try and protect her and get you to step up in that role without blowing my own cover. Looks like it's worked. Regarding Katrina and the Maoli Lodge, it was never supposed to be a location to traffic drugs. But then Joseph Sizemore had the misfortune to get involved with Eduardo Julio Nihei as his dealer. It got Sizemore killed and made his widow a target. Julio's crazed brother, Rafael Carlos Nihei, has a fortified compound in Waimea Canyon on Kauai's west side. But with his drug empire disintegrating before his very eyes, he's getting sloppy and even more unstable than usual ever since Julio was killed."

Lawrence sucked in a long breath. "Working as Nihei's right hand, I've gathered enough evidence, along with the Task Force, to put him away for a very long time. Agent Roxanne Yamamoto—who was a friend of mine before I lost my wife and child, when I was doing standard DEA work—added to that pertinent info with her undercover assignment at the lodge. I was able to retrieve that from her laptop before Rafael's thugs could destroy it. I suggest you take a look at the file, which should be very telling and instrumental in bringing a close to the investigation.

"Well, I better get out of here now, unless I want Nihei to catch me in the act. Not a good idea." He furrowed his brow. "We're not likely to speak face-to-face, Adair, till this thing is over. Either that, or I'll already be dead from overplaying my hand. In which case, guess this would be goodbye and sorry we couldn't meet under better circumstances."

Dex watched him give a mock salute and the video ended as he stared at the empty screen in unadulterated disbelief. Had his assumptions about Lawrence just been turned upside down? Was he actually trying, like himself, to keep Katrina from being harmed rather than the other way around? While pondering this unexpected twist in the investigation, Dex placed a video call to Rachel on the laptop.

"Hey," she said routinely, from her office.

"Is it true that Special Agent Zachary Lawrence is deep undercover as a drug trafficker on Kauai?"

Rachel blinked as she exhaled. "Yes, it's true."

Dex frowned. "Would've appreciated a heads-up about this while conducting our investigation."

"That wasn't possible," she insisted. "You know how it works. We never expose operatives at work, jeopardizing their lives and missions. It was up to Lawrence to decide if and when he was ready to break his cover, which has proven to be invaluable in infiltrating criminal organizations and drug cartels as a credible DEA agent gone bad. Apparently, that time is now."

Dex waited a beat, before conceding that Lawrence did everything the right way. Even if the current investigation had become much more personal to carry out, with the strong feelings Dex had for Katrina. But he was still loyal to the DEA and its objectives. As a result, he needed to see this through to completion. "Is there anything else I need to know?" he asked respectfully.

"Only that I want you and Lawrence, along with Krause and Ishikawa, to work together in your respective capacities to bring down the drug-trafficking ring on Kauai, on behalf of our fallen agent Roxanne Yamamoto, and others affected by this thing in Hawaii and the mainland." The special agent in charge peered at him. "Are we clear?"

"Yeah, we're clear." Dex knew when to quit while he was ahead, knowing there were other issues on the table that needed his focus. Including seeing what information Roxanne had gathered and left behind for them to make use of in breaking up the crime syndicate. "I'll be in touch," he said evenly.

"I'll be waiting." Rachel nodded as if expecting no less of him. "See you soon."

Dex opened the file labeled "DEA Agent Roxanne Yamamoto." It contained a video and a Word document. He held his breath while clicking on the video, wondering what his friend had to say from the grave that, in the words of Agent Lawrence, "should be very telling and instrumental" to the case.

"LOVE YOUR FURNISHINGS," Lynda said, after Katrina welcomed her into the loft and made them Japanese green tea. "I could use some similar pieces to spruce up my condo in LA."

"Thanks." She smiled at her, while wondering if the attractive DEA agent was merely being polite. After all, Katrina was pretty sure that essentially acting as a babysitter for a grown woman, whom her fellow agent Dex was romantically involved with, probably wasn't in her job description. Still, Katrina was grateful to have her there to help safeguard against any possible attack by Zachary Lawrence. "If you're serious, I'd be happy to show you where I purchased them."

Lynda ran a hand through her short hair and responded, "Yeah, definitely. It would be a good way to impress my real significant other, Martin O'Sullivan, who works for the LA County Sheriff's Department."

Katrina chuckled. "And to think, you and Agent Ishikawa seemed like such an item," she teased her.

"We do make a good team." Lynda laughed and sipped her tea as she stood next to the kitchen island. "Maybe in another universe, but not this one. Besides, after going down the aisle twice unsuccessfully, Ishikawa isn't exactly every girl's dream for a guy to bring home to mommy, sweet as he may be when not on the job. Never mind that my own mother has been dead for more than a decade now."

"Do you think that Dex is a good catch to bring home?" Katrina tossed out from the other side of the island and almost immediately wished she could take it back. If only because she wasn't sure just how much his colleagues knew, or wanted to know, about Dex's personal life. On the other hand, maybe this was a good gauge to see where things stood between them from someone in his inner circle.

"Actually, I think Dex is a great catch for someone," Lynda said straightforwardly. "He's been burned once, but is a stand-up guy and knows what he wants in a mate."

"Does he?" Katrina gave her a curious look, as she tasted the tea. *Do I fit the bill?* she asked herself.

"You hit the spot perfectly in that vein," Lynda pointed out. "I can see that Dex is crazy about you."

"Is he?" She couldn't help but blush because the words were melodious to Katrina's ears.

"Yes." The agent didn't back down.

"I feel the same about him." Katrina figured she might as well put it out there. "But I do worry about whether he'll stick around long enough to give it a go," she admitted in all honestly.

Lynda leaned forward. "Whatever happens between you two once our investigation is over, I'm guessing Dex won't be foolish enough to let you get away."

Katrina beamed with that belief. But she knew

she needed to hear it from Dex to know for sure that having a future together was real and not a mirage.

When there was a knock on the door, Katrina reacted with nervousness. So did Lynda, who was immediately alert and asked, "Are you expecting anyone?"

"Not really," she replied cautiously, "but I do run a lodge, so an employee may need me for one thing or another." Would ex-agent Lawrence, her stalker, be so bold as to try something with a former associate on hand and ready to make an arrest?

As if to make sure it was there, Lynda put a hand on the firearm inside the waistband holster tucked beneath her two-button black blazer. "Why don't you take a look at who's there through the peephole."

Katrina nodded and walked to the door. Her heart raced as she looked out, and then leveled off when she saw Alyson standing there. "It's my assistant manager," she told Lynda.

The strain on her face eased and the agent said, "Let her in."

Katrina opened the door and managed a smile. "Hey, Alyson."

Alyson smiled back. "Just dropped by to make sure you were all right."

"I'm good. You want to come in?"

Alyson shook her head. "Actually, there is a small problem…" she started. "Someone had an accident in the pool. Hit her head…"

"Is it serious?" Katrina swallowed a lump in her throat while considering the possibilities.

"She seems fine now, but I thought you should know." Alyson paused. "I'll just double-check—"

When she began to walk away, Katrina impulsively went after her to discuss it further. She felt Lynda hot on her heels. It was only after they both had left the suite that Katrina noticed someone came up behind the DEA agent and whacked her on the back of the head with the butt of a gun. Lynda went down in a heap, knocked unconscious. Only then did Katrina lock eyes with the assailant. She recognized him from his picture as Rafael Carlos Nihei. Aiming the gun directly at her, he said in a no-nonsense, cold tone of voice, "Nice to finally meet you face-to-face, Katrina."

Chapter Seventeen

It was admittedly painful to Dex to see Agent Roxanne Yamamoto spring back to life via video, in what amounted to her final contribution to the DEA and a dedication that proved to be fatal. But if he had anything to say about it, he would see that her great sacrifice was not all for naught. Homing in on the laptop screen, Dex listened to his late friend and former colleague.

"I'm Agent Roxanne Yamamoto," she started, fear in her voice. "If you're watching this, it probably means my cover has been blown and I'm likely dead. I won't bore you with the mundane details of my assignment in posing as a housekeeper at the Maoli Lodge in Poipu on Kauai, investigating possible drug trafficking. These can be found in the other file, along with what I've been able to uncover thus far. Here, I mainly want to say that while working for the lodge, I have seen no evidence whatsoever that its proprietor, Katrina Sizemore, is involved in any way in the trafficking of drugs in and out of her property."

Dex was happy to see that they had reached the same conclusions about Katrina, as Roxanne sucked in a deep breath and continued, "But unfortunately, I have been able to find a secondary connection between the lodge and drug traffickers. Turns out that Katrina's late husband, Joseph Sizemore, was using drugs when he hooked up with drug dealer Eduardo Julio Nihei. Seems like Nihei, along with his brother, Rafael Carlos Nihei, a local drug kingpin, sought to leverage this to use the Maoli Lodge for distributing drugs. It appears as though Sizemore balked and paid for it with his life."

Roxanne ran a finger across a thin brow. "The story doesn't end there," she said contemplatively. "Not even Sizemore's death stopped the Nihei brothers from targeting the lodge as a portal for their illicit drug business. Rafael managed to find someone on the inside to charm into working for his interests. That would be Katrina's assistant manager Alyson Tennison, who, by all accounts, seemed to have fallen head over heels for the drug dealer, based on my surveillance. I haven't been able to warn Katrina yet, without putting her life and mine in danger, but that's my top priority. More later…"

As the video ended, Dex was left with his mouth agape, shocked to learn that someone Katrina obviously trusted was stabbing her in the back. Instead of Zachary Lawrence, it was actually Alyson, hidden in clear view, who posed the real threat to Katrina's safety. Along with the drug trafficker Alyson was romantically involved with, Rafael Carlos Nihei.

I've got to warn Katrina and Lynda, Dex thought anxiously, as he took out his cell phone. Before he could make a move, the phone rang. It was Lynda. He put her on video chat. "Katrina's been kidnapped!" she spoke frantically, with Ishikawa by her side.

Dex's heart pounded loudly in his ears with those frightening words. "What?"

"Her assistant, Alyson, came to the suite," Lynda explained. "Gave her some song and dance about a swimming pool incident. When Katrina stepped out of the room, I followed and someone hit me from behind. I think it might have been Lawrence."

"It wasn't," Dex told her confidently, getting to his feet. "Special Agent Zachary Lawrence is clean. He's been working in a deep uncover capacity."

Lynda gasped with surprise. "If it wasn't him, then I must have been clocked by—"

Dex frowned. "Rafael Carlos Nihei."

"Nihei must have been the one I saw shove Katrina into the back of a pearl beige metallic GMC Yukon Denali," Ishikawa pointed out. "They drove off before I could stop them. I reported the kidnapping and gave the make and model of the vehicle to Detective Pietz, then came back inside to check on Krause and found her unconscious in Katrina's suite."

"I'm fine," Lynda assured him, before Dex could ask, as she put on a brave face. "I always did have a hard head. Guess it came in handy."

"I'm just glad you're okay." Dex wondered if the same could be said for Katrina. The thought of losing her was something he didn't even want to seriously consider. All he knew was that he wasn't about to count on Pietz and the Kauai PD to bring Katrina back to him alive. Dex let Barnabas inside.

"What's the connection between Alyson and Nihei?" Ishikawa asked interestedly.

"Turns out, the two apparently are romantically involved," Dex responded sourly, wondering if Katrina had suspected anything about her double-dealing assistant.

"Alyson sure fooled me," Lynda grumbled. "I should've seen this coming."

"It's no one's fault." He wasn't about to blame her for the assistant manager's conniving and putting on a good act. The important thing was that they find Katrina before it was too late. "I put a GPS tracker on Katrina's phone," Dex told them. Looking at his cell phone, he activated the device, hoping she had left her cell phone on and that the kidnappers hadn't taken or destroyed it. His stomach churned with satisfaction when Dex saw that Katrina's phone was turned on and he could see her location. "They're on the move," he announced, heading out the door. He gave the agents the current location and Dex went after the woman he loved.

"ALYSON'S MY GIRLFRIEND, in case you haven't already put it together," Rafael Carlos Nihei all but bragged to Katrina from where he sat in the front passenger seat of the SUV that she had been forced into the back of at gunpoint. The driver was her stalker, crooked former DEA agent Zachary Lawrence, who had remained mute during the drive, while occasionally making his presence known by glancing in the rearview mirror. Sitting beside Katrina was the woman Rafael was referencing and who had betrayed her: Alyson Tennison. Katrina glared at her assistant manager. Alyson was now holding the gun and pointed it at her somewhat precariously. Katrina found it hard to fathom that the Alyson she thought she knew would have allowed herself to get attached to the wanted and dangerous drug trafficker. Rafael laughed, as though reading her thoughts. "Even you must admit that Alyson played her part well as the devoted employee who never quite got the respect she deserved from you."

"That's not true." Katrina pushed back on that premise. "I always respected you and your role with the Maoli Lodge."

"Yeah, right." Alyson rolled her eyes with a disdain Katrina had never seen before. "Neither you nor Joseph ever gave me the credit I was due for keeping the lodge running smoothly for the most part. You were far too busy sniping at one another or otherwise taking me for granted. I couldn't take it anymore."

"And so, what? This is payback—getting in bed

with a drug trafficker and kidnapping me? That doesn't make any sense," Katrina declared, not holding back in giving her a piece of her mind. She only hoped that Lynda hadn't been seriously hurt when Rafael hit her on the back of the head during the abduction.

"Shut up!" Alyson snapped, her eyes slits. "Whatever you may think of Rafael, he's not a bad person, unless provoked. He provides a needed service that people like your dead husband asked for. If only Joseph hadn't played on his worst instincts, he might be alive today. Think about that!"

Does she really believe that? Katrina drew a disbelieving breath as she considered the toxic words, while conceding that there was a ring of truth to them. But that hardly justified the actions apparently taken in fueling his drug habit. Anger filled her eyes. "Was Joseph murdered?" She needed to know, even as Katrina took note of where they were headed. It seemed to be toward the north shore. Dex had put the tracker on her phone, which she kept on in the back pocket of her high-waist skinny pants. He must surely know by now that she'd been abducted and had some sense of her whereabouts.

When Alyson suddenly went speechless, Rafael said in a callous voice, "He left us no choice but to take him out. When your husband refused to play ball in letting us use the lodge for business, he had to go, to send a message to others who were uncooperative. Joseph's plan to go kayaking was the perfect

means. Giving him just enough fentanyl-laced meth
to make sure he never survived the outing, meant no
more interfering with our agenda."

Katrina put hands to her mouth as the truth settled
in. The idea that Joseph had been the victim of foul
play hit her like a ton of bricks. The fact that Alyson
played a role made it all the more devastating. And
what were their plans for her? Did she truly want to
know? *Keep a cool head*, Katrina told herself, realizing it might be her only chance for surviving this
ordeal. "I suppose it was you who ordered the hit on
my housekeeper, Roxanne?" she addressed the question to the drug trafficker, pretending not to know
Roxanne was a DEA agent, while hoping to buy time
and that somehow Dex would manage to come to her
rescue. Or other law enforcement.

Rafael never wavered in his response, admitting
flat out, "Agent Yamamoto got what was coming to
her. Once Alyson discovered what she was up to as
an undercover investigator for the DEA, overhear-
ing on the phone, we needed to know what she knew,
before soliciting the services of a greedy ex-con to
tamper with her brake lines."

Katrina shot Alyson an icy stare, knowing she
bore the blame for Roxanne's murder. And perhaps
for her own as well, if the traffickers had their way.
"Don't look at me like that," Alyson blared, putting
the gun up to her face. "I never asked Roxanne to
stick her nose where it didn't belong. That's the price
she had to pay."

Katrina withdrew her gaze, not willing to put the battle of wills to the test. Alyson pulled the gun back. Still, she couldn't help but ask the trio, "Whose idea was it to bring cocaine disguised as a cake to my lodge?"

Alyson snarled at her. "I thought it was worth trying to see if we could make this a regular thing," she hissed. "I didn't count on Dex coming in the lounge to play the piano on what was supposed to be his off day. Or that damned dog of his with an uncanny ability to pick up the scent of the cocaine. That's when we knew Dex had to be part of a DEA K-9 unit, along with his supposed pet Barnabas."

Katrina didn't deny it. Nor did she wish to push their buttons any more by praising what Dex and other law enforcement had done in thwarting the drug traffickers' plans.

"Cost my brother, Julio, his life!" Rafael bristled, angling his face at her. "And a valued soldier in Laurie Hoapili. For that, they'll pay…"

The ambiguity of the comment shook Katrina to the core. Was he planning to go after Dex in particular? The DEA? Or the entire Task Force? "Where are you taking me?" she decided to ask, for more stalling, as they drove down Kuhio Highway, believing they would have already killed her by now if Rafael and Zachary Lawrence had wanted to.

"To the airport, if you must know," Zachary spoke for the first time. "With the feds and locals breathing down our necks, we're getting out of Dodge—or off the island—and merely taking you along as an insurance policy in case your DEA pals try to stop us."

"And what then?" Katrina shuddered to think of anything but the worst-case scenario.

"Once we're onboard and there's no trouble, we'll let you go unharmed," he said convincingly. Only she wasn't convinced in the slightest that Rafael—or even Alyson, for that matter—had any intentions of letting her go free. Given that she saw their faces and knew their names, Katrina sensed that she was a dead woman if Dex and company could not reach her in time. Scariest yet was the thought of never getting to tell Dex in straightforward terms how much she loved him and wanted to build a life together.

"JUST GOT A TEXT message from Lawrence, confirming that they have Katrina and are heading to the Princeville Airport," Dex said on his cell speaker-phone, the information corresponding with the GPS tracking of Katrina's cell phone. He was passing the information to Lynda and Ishikawa, as Dex roared down Kuhio Highway or Route 560. Beside him was Barnabas, strapped in a dog car seat. "According to the undercover agent, Nihei has at least one airport official on his payroll." Dex guessed that the drug traffickers were planning to escape on a private jet, possibly to Honolulu, where they would try to get lost and rebuild their operation there. And where would this leave Katrina? Dex was certain that she was being kept alive as an abducted hostage, in case one was needed. Afterward, he had no doubt they planned to kill her, leaving behind no living witnesses. *I can't let that happen*, Dex thought, more determined than he had ever been for anything in his life. He would never get over it if Katrina didn't come out of this alive and before things between them truly had a chance to jell. She needed to know how he felt about her, leaving no doubt. And what he wanted to build with her for the future.

"We'll notify the airport authorities and police to be on the lookout for the vehicle," Ishikawa told him, "which we now know is actually registered to Rafael Carlos Nihei."

"Okay," Dex said anxiously. "With any luck, this can end with no blood being shed." *Certainly not that of Katrina*, he mused, but knew he had to prepare for the real possibility that Nihei would use her as a bargaining chip. Should that fail, it wouldn't take much for him to take his frustrations out on Katrina. Without knowing just how many people the drug trafficker had in his pocket and were equipped to do battle, Dex could only hope that Agent Zachary Lawrence was ready to step up in evening the playing field. Even if it meant compromising his cover in order to protect Katrina. Or anyone else at risk.

"A SWAT team is on its way," Lynda informed him.

"Good." Dex was pleased to hear that, but feared it could be too late to save Katrina. "I'll get there first," he told them assuredly, and disconnected.

Pressing down on the accelerator to close the distance between him and the vehicle carrying Katrina, Dex ignored the speed limit and dared anyone to try and stop him. Within minutes, he had reached the private airport, some three nautical miles from Hanalei. Having cleared some hurdles with the help of Clayton Pietz and Rachel Zavatti, Dex was able to go straight through to near the single airstrip, where he spotted the Yukon Denali. The doors were open and Dex could see no one inside. Where the hell were they?

Then he saw a group of five people—including Katrina, who was being held by Rafael Carlos Nihei, followed by Agent Lawrence, Alyson Tennison, and a tall and thickset bald Hawaiian male—headed toward a light jet. Dex recognized it as a Hawker 400XP. He got out of his own car, along with Barnabas, determined to stop them from boarding the aircraft at all costs. Taking out his Glock 27 pistol, Dex approached the group and yelled at Nihei, "Let her go!"

The drug kingpin turned toward Dex and immediately grabbed Katrina around the neck from behind while whipping out his own firearm and holding it to her head. "I don't think so, Agent Adair. Your girlfriend's coming with us. Back off!"

"It's over, Nihei." Dex's voice was commanding. "I suggest you and your cronies do yourselves a favor and give up the fight. This place will be swarming with law enforcement any moment now. You're never going to get off the island."

"We'll see about that!" Nihei pressed the gun to Katrina's temple. "Try and stop us and she dies, right before your very eyes."

Dex sized up the situation. He knew there were three actual perpetrators against two good guys— him and, he believed, Lawrence. With backup about to join them. He wasn't willing to wait that long, at risk to Katrina's life. But making the wrong move could backfire and leave his beloved dead. In a split second, Dex watched as Katrina took matters into her own hands. She grabbed her kidnapper's wrist and moved the gun away from her face and into the air as a shot went off. She then slammed her foot as hard as she could into Nihei's ankle.

He let out a loud scream and tried to regain control as Katrina squatted. Dex wasn't about to give him that chance. Using the clear view of his face, he fired a single shot that hit Nihei squarely in the temple, dropping him like a stone and putting his lights out for good. When the bald-headed man, who had removed a firearm, took aim at Dex and fired, it was Lawrence who grabbed his arm just in time to miss by a mile. The agent then landed a roundhouse punch straight to the jaw of the drug trafficker. Though staggered, he managed to get off another shot, hitting Lawrence in the chest, sending him down.

Before the bald assailant could take a second shot at Dex, Barnabas, acting in his dual role as a handler protector, went after him, jumping on him before the unsub could respond, holding him prisoner. Dex moved quickly toward Katrina, who was engaged in battle with Nihei's lover, Alyson. Just when Dex thought he might have to lend her a helping hand, Katrina downed her former assistant manager with a solid punch to the nose, knocking Alyson out cold.

The SWAT team and other law enforcement converged upon the scene, placing Alyson and the bald-headed man under arrest. They surrounded the private jet, preventing the pilot from departing, before taking her into custody.

En route to Katrina, who seemed to have things well under control for the moment, Dex checked on Agent Lawrence, still down. "You okay?"

"Been better, to tell you the truth." Zachary sat up and rubbed the Hawaiian shirt with plumerias covering his chest. "Fortunately, I always wear a bulletproof vest, as I'm sure you do, when on the job."

"Always." Dex gave him a nod of respect. "Have to admit, Lawrence, you had me going for a while there."

"Had the situations been reversed, I would've had my own doubts about you." Zachary winced. "But we both chose this life and have to go with the flow."

"Yeah." Dex was thoughtful.

"Better go see about Katrina. She needs you right now more than I do."

Dex nodded and headed toward her. Katrina ran

into Dex's arms, both clinging to each other for a long moment. "Did they hurt you?" he asked.

"No, but I have a feeling they planned to kill me had this thing gone south," she said honestly.

"I wouldn't have let that happen." Dex cupped her dimpled chin and kissed her lips. "Not in this lifetime."

Katrina glanced over at Zachary, who was now on his feet and conversing with Pietz and Ishikawa. "I saw you talking to Zachary Lawrence," she noted.

Dex smiled. "Turns out, he wasn't one of the bad guys after all."

"Yes, he kind of intimated that to me when we had a moment," she stated musingly, "and he apologized about the messages and stalking. I started to really believe him when he stepped in to prevent Nihei's henchman from shooting you. Before Barnabas took over from there."

"Yeah, there was that," Dex acknowledged, knowing he owed Lawrence one. Even if the agent had put them through the paces with his undercover assignment. Just then, Barnabas came running up to them, the golden retriever wagging his tale triumphantly for a job well done in picking up where Lawrence left off in protecting Dex, as intended. He stroked the K-9 cop's neck and said, "Really good job, boy!"

"I second that!" Katrina sang, petting the dog under his chin. "You really did save the day, along with your handler." Barnabas reacted favorably by barking his approval and lapping up the attention.

"You did good, too," he praised her. "Frustrating Nihei and giving me just the space I needed to take him out."

She chuckled. "Figured I needed to do something to come out of this in one piece."

Dex laughed, loving the camaraderie between them as a trio and wanting to keep it going for as long as possible. He became serious again as he cast his eyes upon Katrina, musing about the way things turned out with her assistant manager. "I'm sorry that Alyson betrayed your trust."

"Me too." Katrina winced. "She'll likely have a pretty sore, if not broken, nose for a while, and plenty of time to think about all the problems she's brought upon herself."

"You're right." He was glad that Katrina knew how to handle herself in a pinch. "Shouldn't be too hard to find a new and reliable assistant manager," he imagined.

"I suppose." She held his hands. "Apart from that, you and I make a great team, Dex, even when danger was swirling all around us like a vortex."

"Agreed." He grinned, and decided now was as good a time as any to make his pitch. "I'd like to make our teamwork even better," he told her. "I'm in love with you, Katrina. I have some money saved up and would love to go into early retirement and become your partner in running the Maoli Lodge. And eventually make a go of it as husband and wife. I know that's a lot to take in. If you need time to think about it, that's perfectly understandable."

"I don't need to think about it," she professed. "Yes and yes, Dex! I'd love to go into partnership with you as co-owners of the Maoli Lodge. And it would be my honor to marry the man I've fallen in love with and have him as my future husband." Katrina paused, gazing into his eyes doubtfully. "Are you sure you're ready to give up working as a DEA special agent?"

"More than I've ever been about anything in my life—" Dex spoke from the heart "—with the exception of the deep love I feel for you."

"Good answer." She grinned. "In that case, shall we seal the deal with another kiss?"

"Absolutely," he laughed. Dex was more than happy to take the lead on this one, before giving way to a lifetime of equality in matters of love and the successful operation of a lodge in the Poipu resort on the island of Kauai, Hawaii.

Epilogue

The raid on Rafael Carlos Nihei's compound in Waimea Canyon, netted the DEA large quantities of crystal methamphetamine and fentanyl, drug paraphernalia, illegal firearms and cash. Several members of the slain leader's drug network were arrested as a result, putting a serious dent into the illicit drug-trafficking operation between the island, other parts of Hawaii and the mainland. This was eight months ago and Dex's last assignment as a DEA special agent, before entering into voluntary retirement, along with his trusted canine companion, Barnabas. After selling his Los Angeles home, they resettled in Poipu. Joining forces with his gorgeous wife, Katrina, in operating the Maoli Lodge—where he also shared piano duties with new mom, Gina Oxenberg—was the smartest move Dex believed he'd ever made. Next to marrying the crimson-haired beauty.

To say he didn't miss being a federal law enforcement agent in the slightest would be dishonoring the men and women he worked with in going after drug traffickers, crime syndicates and related wrongdoers. On the contrary, Dex had no problem going through the withdrawal pains of absence from the DEA as part of the natural process. But that was easily over-come by being in the daily company of the love of his life in Katrina. He was already looking forward to the day when their attempt to get pregnant would be successful and they could welcome a girl or boy into the world to love as much as they did one another.

THE KAUAI MARATHON and Half Marathon was held in September and Katrina was proud to be a partic-ipant, along with her husband, Dex. With her love for running and adventure, she considered it a great way to do both, while tapping into his desire to stay in shape in the post DEA era for him. At the same time, Katrina was doing her best to help as he made the transition from special agent to a married man, leaving behind his LA life to make a new one with her in paradise on Kauai. Luckily, Dex was all in, embracing the challenge of stepping out of his com-fort zone and into the Hawaiian experience of run-ning in the spirit of community, passing by Taiko drum troupes and exotic hula dancers along the way.

"I think running could become a regular part of my routine," Dex told her, grinning, "as long as I can continue to keep up with you."

Katrina chuckled, gazing at him in his T-shirt and sweat shorts, muscles bulging in his arms and legs. "Something tells me you'll have no problem in that department." She warmed to the thought of their lovemaking and the ability to keep up with each other. Wearing a sports bra and running shorts, with her red hair in a high ponytail, Katrina winked and ran ahead of Dex. She fought hard to wait until they got back to their suite in the lodge, before she sprang on Dex what she had just discovered herself. "Just so you know, you're going to be a dad."

His eyes lit with delight. "Are you saying what I think you are?"

She broke into a huge smile, knowing he wanted this as much as she did. "Yes, Dex, we're having a baby!"

Katrina's husband cried as he wrapped her in his arms and swirled her around. "You've just made me the happiest man in the world."

"And you've made me the happiest woman on the planet," she proclaimed, "so there."

They kissed on that treasured emotion and were already starting to pick out names for the new addition to the Adair family.

* * * * *

Look for more books in R. Barri Flowers's series,
Hawaii CI, coming soon.

And if you missed the first book in the series,
The Big Island Killer *is available now wherever*
Harlequin Intrigue books are sold!

WE HOPE YOU ENJOYED
THIS BOOK FROM
⊕HARLEQUIN

INTRIGUE

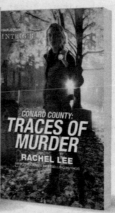

Seek thrills. Solve crimes. Justice served.

Dive into action-packed stories that will keep you
on the edge of your seat. Solve the crime
and deliver justice at all costs.

6 NEW BOOKS AVAILABLE EVERY MONTH!

#2103 CONARD COUNTY: CHRISTMAS CRIME SPREE
Conard County: The Next Generation • by Rachel Lee

Savage attacks on several women in parson Molly Canton's parish threaten the holiday season. Assisting Detective Callum McCloud's investigation, Molly is drawn to the tortured man. But once the detective realizes these attacks are a smoke screen obscuring the real target—Molly—the stakes escalate...especially now that Molly's goodness has breached Callum's calloused heart.

#2104 POLICE DOG PROCEDURAL
K-9s on Patrol • by Lena Diaz

When police lieutenant Macon Ridley and his K-9, Bogie, respond to a call from Daniels Canine Academy, they discover a baby on DCA's doorstep. Even more surprising, the chemistry that sizzled when Macon first met Emma Daniels sparks once again. Now, not only is an innocent infant's life at stake but so is Emma's...

#2105 EAGLE MOUNTAIN CLIFFHANGER
Eagle Mountain Search and Rescue • by Cindi Myers

Responding to the reports of a car accident, newcomer Deputy Jake Gwynn finds a murder scene instead. Search and rescue paramedic Hannah Richards tried to care for the likely suspect before he slipped away—and now he's gone from injured man to serial killer on the loose. And she's his next target.

#2106 SMALL TOWN VANISHING
Covert Cowboy Soldiers • by Nicole Helm

Rancher Brody Thompson's got a knack for finding things, even in the wild and remote Wyoming landscape he's just begun to call home. So when Kate Phillips asks for Brody's help in solving her father's decade-old disappearance, he's intrigued. But there's a steep price to pay for uncovering the truth...

#2107 PRESUMED DEAD
Defenders of Battle Mountain • by Nichole Severn

Forced to partner up, reserve officer Kendric Hudson and missing persons agent Campbell Dwyer work a baffling abduction case that gets more dangerous with each new revelation. As they battle a mounting threat, they must also trust one another with their deepest secrets.

#2108 WYOMING WINTER RESCUE
Cowboy State Lawmen • by Juno Rushdan

Trying to stop a murderous patient has consumed psychotherapist Lynn Delgado. But when a serial killer targets Lynn, she must accept protection and turn to lawman Nash Garner for help. As she flees the killer in a raging blizzard, Nash follows, risking everything to save the woman he's falling for.

The whole desperate plan began simply as a last-ditch attempt to save his life. He never intended for anyone to get hurt. That day, not long after Thanksgiving, he walked into the bank full of hope. It was the first time he'd ever asked for a loan. It was also the first time he'd ever seen executive loan officer Carla Richmond.

When he tapped at her open doorway, she looked up from that big desk of hers. He thought she was too young and pretty with her big blue eyes and all that curly chestnut-brown hair to make the decision as to whether he lived or died.

She had a great smile as she got to her feet to offer him a seat.

He felt so out of place in her plush office that he stood in the doorway nervously kneading the brim of his worn baseball cap for a moment before stepping in. As he did, her blue-eyed gaze took in his ill-fitting clothing hanging on his rangy body, his bad haircut, his large, weathered hands.

He told himself that she'd already made up her mind before he even sat down. She didn't give men like him a second look—let alone money. Like his father always said, bankers never gave dough to poor people who actually needed it. They just helped their rich friends.

Right away Carla Richmond made him feel small with her questions about his employment record, what he had for collateral, why he needed the money and how he planned to repay it. He'd recently lost one crappy job and was in the process of starting another temporary one, and all he had to show for the years he'd worked hard labor since high school was an old pickup and a pile of bills.

He took the forms she handed him and thanked her, knowing he wasn't going to bother filling them in. On the way out of her office, he balled them up and dropped them in the trash. All the way to his pickup, he mentally kicked himself for being such a fool. What had he expected?

No one was going to give him money, even to save his life—especially some woman in a suit behind a big desk in an air-conditioned office. It didn't matter that she didn't have a clue how desperate he really was. All she'd seen when she'd looked at him was a loser. To think that he'd bought a new pair of jeans with the last of his cash and borrowed a too-large button-up shirt from a former coworker for this meeting.

After climbing into his truck, he sat for a moment, too scared and sick at heart to start the engine. The worst part was the thought of going home and telling Jesse. The way his luck was going, she would walk out on him. Not that he could blame her, since his gambling had gotten them into this mess.

He thought about blowing off work, since his new job was only temporary anyway, and going straight to the bar. Then he reminded himself that he'd spent the last of his money on the jeans. He couldn't even afford a beer. His own fault, he reminded himself. He'd only made things worse when he'd gone to a loan shark for cash and then stupidly gambled the money, thinking he could make back what he owed and then some when he won. He'd been so sure his luck had changed for the better when he'd met Jesse.

Last time the two thugs had come to collect the interest on the loan, they'd left him bleeding in the dirt outside his rented house. They would be back any day.

With a curse, he started the pickup. A cloud of exhaust blew out the back as he headed home to face Jesse with the bad news. Asking for a loan had been a long shot, but still he couldn't help thinking about the disappointment he'd see in her eyes when he told her. They'd planned to go out tonight for an expensive dinner with the loan money to celebrate.

As he drove home, his humiliation began to fester like a sore that just wouldn't heal. Had he known even then how this was going to end? Or was he still telling himself he was just a nice guy who'd made some mistakes, had some bad luck and gotten involved with the wrong people?

Get 4 FREE REWARDS!

We'll send you 2 FREE Books plus 2 FREE Mystery Gifts.

FREE Value Over **$20**

Both the **Harlequin Intrigue®** and **Harlequin® Romantic Suspense** series feature compelling novels filled with heart-racing action-packed romance that will keep you on the edge of your seat.

HARLEQUIN
PLUS

Announcing a **BRAND-NEW** multimedia subscription service for romance fans like you!

Read, Watch and Play.

Experience the easiest way to get the romance content you crave.

Start your **FREE 7 DAY TRIAL** at
<u>www.harlequinplus.com/freetrial</u>.